Kim
Beach Brides Series

by

Magdalena Scott

Kim

Beach Brides Series

Copyright 2017 - Magdalena Scott

Trade Paperback Release July 2017
ISBN-10:0-9971922-4-0
ISBN-13:978-0-9971922-4-7

Published by Jewel Box Books
Edited by Karen Block

Cover Design by Raine English,
www.ElusiveDreamsDesigns.com

Introduction

Grab your beach hat and a towel and prepare for a brand new series brought to you by twelve *New York Times* and *USA Today* bestselling authors...

Beach Brides! Fun in the summer sun!

Twelve heartwarming, sweet novellas linked by a unifying theme.
You'll want to read each one!

BEACH BRIDES SERIES (Kim)
Twelve friends from the online group, Romantic Hearts Book Club, decide to finally meet in person during a destination Caribbean vacation to beautiful Enchanted Island. While of different ages and stages in life, these ladies have two things in common: 1) they are diehard romantics, and 2) they've been let down by love. As a wildly silly dare during her last night on the island, each heroine decides to stuff a note in a bottle addressed to her "dream hero" and cast it out to sea! Sending a message in a bottle can't be any crazier than online or cell phone dating, or

posting personal ads! And, who knows? One of these mysterious missives might actually lead to love...

Join Meg, Tara, Nina, Clair, Jenny, Lisa, Hope, Kim, Rose, Lily, Faith and Amy, as they embark on the challenge of a lifetime: risking their hearts to accomplish their dreams.

This is Kim's story....

Jon was engaged when he "landed" the message in a bottle on a fishing trip, and it disappeared before he could decide whether to respond. Now unattached, he's on a road trip with Kim, whose gratitude in spite of a painful past reminds him of the touching note he wishes he'd kept.

Meet the Beach Brides:

MEG (Julie Jarnagin)
TARA (Ginny Baird)
NINA (Stacey Joy Netzel)
CLAIR (Grace Greene)
JENNY (Melissa McClone)
LISA (Denise Devine)

HOPE (Aileen Fish)

KIM (Magdalena Scott)

ROSE (Shanna Hatfield)

LILY (Ciara Knight)

FAITH (Helen Scott Taylor)

AMY (Raine English)

Prologue

Kim's message in a bottle...

I'M WRITING THIS letter under protest, because a bunch of my friends are each writing one. And no, I don't need to hear the old question, "If your friends were jumping off a cliff, would you jump too?"

Answer: No. But I would write this silly letter.

FYI—I don't expect this bottle to be found by the man of my dreams. Though I've had some rocky times, I am not desperate for romance.

I have a great career, friends, and a life I enjoy. I'm considering adopting a pet. So, you can see, when you read this sometime in the future, I'll probably be much too busy and happy to become involved with you.

This is just fair warning, because I am an extremely honest person. If you are married, please burn or shred this note. Or you can seal it back in the bottle and chuck it into the ocean again, if you're the romantic type.

If you are not married or in a relationship and want to be my email pen pal, I might be open to that. But nothing more. I expect we have zero in common beyond a possible scientific curiosity, re: bottle floating from where I tossed it to wherever you found it.

Makes me think, for some reason, of Star Wars. *Are you a fan of sci fi?*

Do you believe people are fated to certain experiences?

And do you believe it's important to stand by someone even when leaving is immeasurably easier? If your answer to this question is "no," please forget this bottle came into your life.

Yours truly (because how else should I close this?)

whitecapkr@...

P.S. The girls are watching to make sure I fill up the page. Otherwise I would have written less.

Like this:

Hi. I don't believe you're out there.

Chapter One

THE PATIO OF Tony's Macaroni in Serendipity, Indiana, was busy tonight. Kim Rose sipped her red wine, letting it slide down her throat as she anticipated a delicious meal. The weather was perfect. A warm breeze teased her with the rich, spicy smell of the neighboring table's lasagna. She glanced at a couple nearby who seemed to be in a romantic world of their own.

When a car horn honked, her friend, Emily Standish, sitting across the table from her, raised a hand in a wave.

A puff of wind blew some hair into Kim's eyes. She pulled a scrunchie out of her handbag and jerked her hair into a ponytail, hoping all of it would stay under control for once.

"Emily, do you know who that was? Or did you just wave *in case* you knew?"

Emily laughed. "Her name is Lauren. One of her sisters was in my high school class."

Kim shook her head in amazement. "I'm not sure I'll ever get used to living in a small town. You seem to have a connection to everyone in Serendipity."

Emily leaned back in her chair, smiling. "That's one result of living in the same place all my life. But, Kim, you know more people every day." Emily tipped her head, concerned. "I hope you're not second-guessing your decision to move here."

Kim put a hand over her friend's. "Not second-guessing. I'm just still in the adjustment period." For years, Kim had lived and worked in New Albany, Indiana, a vibrant community minutes away from the culture, shopping, and dining opportunities of Louisville, Kentucky. Except for the incredible speed of the gossip tree, everything in Serendipity moved at a slower pace than Kim was accustomed to. "Serendipity has a very different lifestyle. I'm learning how it works."

Emily nodded. "Remember when I told you that Serendipity Hospital was looking for nurses? I warned you of what to expect here."

"Yes, ma'am, I remember, and I told you I was ready for a drastic change. I love Serendipity. I feel happier than I have in a long time." She sipped more wine, to shut herself up and avoid getting maudlin about the past. "I'll have to be okay with the possibility that I'll never know as many people as you do. Sometimes I think you can call every one of Serendipity's six thousand citizens by name."

Emily cringed. "In my sordid past, I probably called a few of them some names I shouldn't have. Good thing you dragged me down the road to recovery after my car wreck and helped me change my attitude." She shook her head in dismay. "Sometimes I can't believe how rotten I was back in the day."

Kim laughed, glad for the change in subject. Before becoming a nurse, she was an aid in the facility where Emily was sent for physical therapy and rehabilitation. At first, nobody wanted to be around the angry, bitter young woman. "You were certainly one of our most well-known patients."

Emily covered her eyes with her hands and shook her head. Her words were muffled when she spoke. "Okay, I'm really wishing for some brain bleach here. Thank goodness I wasn't a lost cause."

"Nobody is a lost cause," Kim said. That belief was important to her sanity at work, and she had to believe it for herself.

Emily removed her hands and leaned forward, elbows on the table. "Do you ever think about all the connections in our lives, things that happen and we don't realize the importance until later?"

Kim slowly twirled her wineglass on the table, wishing for the food to arrive or for someone to recognize Emily and interrupt their conversation. Anything. "What kind of connections do you mean?"

Emily's eyes sparkled. "Well, my wreck for one. It was a terrible thing, for me, for my family. But so much good has come out of it."

Kim had a flash of Emily's wedding day. "Your relationship with David sure evolved during your rehab."

"Absolutely. He and I wouldn't have gotten together otherwise. But so many things led up to that. And, Kim, getting to know you was a big life changer. You taught me a lot about gratitude and about working hard to achieve a worthwhile goal."

Kim laughed. "I did? Really, I was just trying to keep you from giving up on yourself."

Her friend shook a finger at her. "Don't shrug it off, Kim. I'm serious. Your attitude toward life after losing your mom to breast cancer and going through that yourself—and the boyfriend who dumped you—"

Kim slid down in her chair and whispered, "You're making me feel pretty awesome right now."

Emily frowned. "I don't mean to be negative. I'm talking about being grateful every day even when life is hard. That's what you taught me, Kim."

I'd love an instant replay of those lessons. The audio version so I can listen on my phone whenever I need a lift.

Kim cleared her throat. "New topic. The road trip. Are you one hundred percent sure you can't go?"

An unusual look passed quickly over Emily's face. "Yes. One hundred percent. I'd love to see that area, and I will someday. But I want to make it a family vacation. Something David and I do together and take Isabel when she's old enough to enjoy it. I know you're eager to go, and you're just being kind."

"Well, I am looking forward to it, but I'd step aside and let you go. I wouldn't know Travis and Suzanne without you introducing me. If you were up for it, we could both go. Surely there's room in their car for four. Not sure about four plus a car seat." She chuckled at her own joke.

Emily coughed, seemed to narrowly avoid spitting wine. "Oops. Excuse me—wine went down the wrong way."

She replaced her glass on the table, just as Tony, the restaurant co-owner, appeared with their handmade pizza. It was beautiful and smelled heavenly.

He set it on the table with a flourish. "You ladies need anything else right now?"

Emily looked at Kim and answered for both of them. "We're good, Tony. Thanks. It's a perfect night to eat on the patio. I'm so glad you added this."

He shook his head, chuckling. "Thanks. It hurts to admit it was the wife's idea, and I kept telling her nobody'd be interested. I'll be eating crow about that for the rest of my life, I guess."

"If you get to do that on the patio, it won't be so bad."

Tony covered his ears, laughing. "Yeah, yeah, yeah." He excused himself and checked in with another table.

Emily served a slice of pizza to Kim and put one on her own plate. "Back to the road trip. It's all yours, Kim. Have a great time. Take loads of photos and text them to me. I know you're ready for a break. You haven't taken a real vacation since that island trip with your book club friends, right?"

Kim chewed slowly, picturing scenes from Enchanted Island. "Yes. It's almost two years. Hard to believe. We were chatting about it online the other night."

And even harder to believe that some of the girls had actually met the men of their dreams through that ridiculous bottle toss. She hadn't told anybody outside the group about the message in a bottle. Not even Emily. Emily would probably have a good laugh about it if she heard, and Kim wasn't ready to provide that comic relief.

Kim was realistic. She didn't expect a knight in shining armor to sweep her onto his galloping white steed and carry her off to live in a castle. She had to do the best she could with the life she had, and that meant learning, again, to be grateful each day. And being satisfied with experiencing romance by reading about it in novels. The real-life kind was too painful to risk again.

Gratitude changes lives, she'd heard. Evidently, she'd said it a few times, and Emily had paid attention. Maybe it was time Kim re-learned the lessons she had taught her friend.

Nobody is a lost cause. Not even me.

Chapter Two

JON WHITFIELD LOADED suitcases into his friend Travis's car. Yesterday he'd driven from the foothills of the Smoky Mountains to Travis and Suzanne's house in Nashville, Tennessee. He'd left his Corvette in their garage, and he and Travis had taken turns driving to a hotel in southern Indiana where the three of them spent the night.

Travis's wife, Suzanne, six months pregnant, appreciated and needed the addition of a hotel stay to the trip itinerary. If Jon had been making this journey alone, he'd be hours further along. But, then again, if he were going alone to this machine fabricating conference in Minneapolis, Minnesota, he would have flown instead. He was uneasy about being away from the factory for the additional time that driving required.

"Suzanne, how are you handling the trip?" Jon asked when Travis pulled out of the hotel parking lot.

She settled into her seat and smiled. "Great. I'm really enjoying the scenery. Everything is so lush and green. This two-lane highway to Serendipity will be beautiful—wooded areas, fields of corn, soybeans, whatever. And neat homes. I wouldn't want to live anywhere but Nashville but can see why David and Emily love it here."

Travis increased his speed to fifty-five when they left the little town, though he had to slow often for curves. "I'm sure glad to be done with the interstate for a while. But don't worry, Jon. We'll make up time when we get on the next one."

Jon picked up his phone. "I'll let David know we're only about an hour away. I want to be sure he has time to kick a path through the house before we get there."

Travis laughed. "That was the old days, buddy. Haven't you visited since he and Emily got married?"

Jon paused, considered rewording the text. "Been busy. You know the drill."

"Sure, but you know. Friends?" Travis shook his head. "Emily has that house looking great. Even now that they have Isabel, it's so neat you won't recognize it. Emily and Suzanne have that in common. Right, honey?"

Suzanne patted her tummy. "I hope to be as good a mom as Emily is. I assume she used a front-end loader to transform David's house into a home."

Jon finished the text, which no longer included the phrase *kick a path*. He hit send. "Does that mean you can't build forts with pizza boxes anymore?"

Suzanne and Travis both laughed.

Jon watched the rural scenery slide past. He felt bad that he hadn't visited David since the wedding. And he felt like a heel for trying to talk Travis out of this side trip. There were a couple of reasons. One was the stated busyness. He'd taken a big chance by leaving a successful company to take over a struggling, large machine shop in little Legend, Tennessee. His income was drastically lower and he had more responsibilities than ever, but he knew if things went right, he could make a difference for a lot of people.

If this conference hadn't been so important, he'd have stayed home and worked. This was the first time since Jon's career shift that he and Travis had both managed to attend the conference. Back in the day, the company they worked for had paid for both of them to attend. Jon was footing his own bill this year and looked forward to both the business networking and the personal reconnections.

The other reason he had avoided Serendipity since Emily and David's wedding was Emily's best friend, Kim. The woman had treated him like pond scum when they met at the wedding and, for some reason, he couldn't get that out of his head. Since then, he'd only seen David at their annual guys' trip with Travis and their other college friends or at someone else's home. Not in Serendipity.

Never before had Jon made an effort to *avoid* a pretty, smart woman. He wouldn't tell the others and knew it was ridiculous, but Kim had made an indelible impression on him, and he didn't know why.

He gave himself a mental shake. This brief stop should be fine; there shouldn't be an opportunity to run into her. They would be at David's only for a couple of hours for a visit over brunch, then hit the road again.

Travis looked in the rearview mirror at his wife. "You still doing okay? Need anything?"

Jon saw Suzanne's eyes roll. "Travis, I'm fine. I'm healthy, well fed, even well-rested for the most part. If I'd realized how much you were going to obsess about me being along, I might have stayed home."

Travis's brows raised. "What? No way. I'd obsess ten times as much if I wasn't with you. This way, you get a little vacation, see some sights. Or you can lie around the hotel room or the pool all day if you want."

Suzanne grinned, her cheeks turning a bit pink when she saw Jon watching her. He wondered if she would be bored stiff the whole time he and Travis were at the conference.

What the couple didn't talk about was the two miscarriages they'd suffered. Travis only told Jon about them when they were preparing to sign up for the conference. He didn't want to leave Suzanne at home, her doctor advised against flying, and the road trip began to evolve.

Jon didn't know much about pregnancy, thank goodness, but for his friends' sake wanted to do everything possible to keep Suzanne well and comfortable.

Travis laughed suddenly, jerking Jon out of his reverie. "Hey, Jonny-boy, tell Suzanne the fishing trip story. You know, when you caught every bit of trash in ten square miles of ocean? I've told her, but I know it'll be a lot funnier if you do your version."

Jon groaned silently. He would never live down that story but, at least, if he told the tale, it wouldn't be as grossly overstated as he knew was currently circulating. Making the miles go past more quickly was an incentive, and by the time they reached David's house, he'd be done with the story.

"Okay, if I must. Suzanne, you know the way your husband and our other so-called friends like to pick on each other? Well, that fishing trip, it seemed to be my turn to be the butt of all jokes." He paused, remembering as if it were yesterday and deciding how to tell it, while omitting what he didn't want to share.

****

Jon pulled with all his might on the industrial-strength fishing pole. Finally, this would be something worth keeping. His buddies had all reeled in a big fish. Some had been photographed and thrown back, but they would be grilling Ryan's catch at their rented condo tonight. Maybe Jon could provide tomorrow's lunch. So far he had only provided laughs for his friends with the array of ocean-garbage he'd snagged his line on.

A few minutes later, Travis, leaning over the rail, started to laugh. "You've outdone yourself this time, Jonny-boy."

He wanted to cut the line right then, knowing there was no fish. Again.

The guys all took out their phones and photographed him while he pulled each item out of the seaweed-entangled remains of an old net. A deflated Mylar balloon, the rings from a pack of aluminum cans, some plastic shopping bags, and a large rubber boot.

Dustin held up the boot with a thumb and forefinger. "I don't know, Jon. Maybe you should keep this boot and try again. With your amazing luck, you might pull in its mate." He handed the slimy boot to Jon, and the phone cameras went off again.

Jon noticed the boot wasn't empty. He wasn't sure he wanted to see what it contained, but curiosity took over. He held it as far from his face as he could to avoid being overwhelmed by the stench and still see what was in it. He pulled out a wine bottle, and the guys started laughing again.

Ryan slapped him on the back. "Hey, Jon, is that a priceless vintage that fell overboard a couple *hundred years ago? That would be almost better than a decent-sized fish."*

No, it wasn't a priceless vintage. The label of a middle-grade winery was mostly gone, and the bottle was stoppered but empty.

Or was it?

Travis grabbed the bottle from Jon and held it aloft. "Oh, wow, check this out. Message in a bottle. Could be your dream girl, Jonny-boy." Brows raised above his laughing eyes, he handed the bottle back and clasped his hands in mock anticipation. "Okay, we're waiting."

Jon felt the heat on his neck. The ribbing was typical, but for some reason, discovering the message in a bottle was something he didn't feel like being jabbed about. "Yeah? Waiting for what?"

Dustin's eyes rolled. "Open it, idiot. Let's see what it says."

Just to shut them up, he worked at the stopper until it finally released. A note, tightly bound with a red hair bungee, slid out. He read it quickly, expecting it to be something ridiculous. But instead, the simple, heartfelt note tugged at his jaded heart. Here was a woman who thought little of herself and didn't expect to find love it seemed, by message in a bottle or any other means. Maybe he was reading between the lines too much. He had a tendency to do that—Andrea told him so plenty of times.

Andrea. Yeah, Jon didn't need to swoon over a note in a bottle. He was engaged to a blond bombshell.

He rolled up the note, secured it with the bungee, slid it back down the throat of the bottle, and replaced the stopper. Then he tossed the bottle aside. It landed with a thud on the pile of garbage he had pulled in during the expensive fishing trip. "Satellite TV ad. Let's go below and get a beer."

The guys were always relentless in picking on each other, and today his poor luck at fishing meant it was his turn to be on the receiving end. It was all part of their typical interplay, and he knew the best defense was to ignore them and divert their attention. Beer was sometimes quite useful for this. A game on TV was another winner, but the fishing boat for tourists off the coast of Florida didn't provide TV. Evidently, they expected the participants to be satisfied with a day on the ocean, camaraderie, food, and drink.

Go figure.

At the highly polished bar below deck, Jon bought a round for everyone and settled into one of the chairs, joining in the conversation about the Cubs' chances of winning the World Series this year. That was much better than thinking about the stupidly romantic idea of a message in a bottle.

In spite of himself, his mind wouldn't let go of the bottle with the piece of paper scrolled inside.

The rest of the fishing excursion was uneventful. Jon didn't try again, opting to cheer his buddies on, leaning against the rail, inhaling the salty air, and being generally awed by the never-ending expanse of the ocean that met the bowl of an intense blue sky. In spite of his lack of fishing luck, today was perfect. Great weather, plenty of good-natured ribbing at his expense, decent food and drink.

He and the guys had done trips together every year for a while now. At the airport when he was waiting for his flight to meet the others, he had fallen into conversation with an elderly gentleman who was on his way to spend a week with his friends. The old man's face was a lined map of his life, and when he spoke of the friends he was going to meet, his eyes sparkled. He had clapped Jon on the shoulder. "The boys and I have been doing this trip every year for forty years, young man. I hope you and your friends will reach that milestone. I'll tell you, it's worth trying."

Jon had muttered something in agreement, in awe of the man and his friends and forty years of making their relationship a priority. How great was that?

Jon would love to achieve such a record, but he didn't know about some of the others. Three of them were married now; one was a dad, and another would be in a few months. Already they had to avoid the birthdays of wives and one child when comparing calendars to schedule their trip. Soon there'd be the complication of even more kids' birthdays and, before long, their sports events. Jon knew the guys wouldn't intentionally let their friendships fade into the background, but that was part of what women did.

Yeah, Jon knew all about how women could change your life. Being in a relationship started out seeming like a good idea, then a great idea. Andrea was gorgeous; he was lucky she was interested in him. But he wasn't sure how they'd ended up engaged.

Was he ready for that commitment? From one day to the next, he didn't know what to expect of her.

Travis punched his shoulder, pulling him back to reality. "What are you dreaming about, Jonny-boy?"

He stood up straight, preparing his rebuff and feeling a slow smile appear. "Just wondered if we could lower you with a rope around your feet and use you as bait for some real fish."

Travis laughed. "Unless somebody else is manning the poles, there's no use in even trying that, Jon. You better be happy with your bottle in a boot and leave the fishing to the real men."

Jon laughed with him. Fishing wasn't the point of the trip. Spending time with his buddies was the point.

When Travis turned back toward the rail, Jon looked at the pile of garbage again. The boot was there, but he couldn't see the bottle. Must have gotten hidden under something else. He'd find a quiet moment later and retrieve the note.

But even after he bought another round of beers downstairs and excused himself to use the "head" then slipped up on deck, he couldn't locate the bottle. Had it somehow been discarded overboard again? Had someone else opened it, read the note, and laughed at it? He shrugged, trying not to care. Trying not to feel he'd just missed the chance of a lifetime. He remembered part of the note, but not the email address. What he knew he'd never forget was the way the woman's words had affected him.

Andrea's face jumped into his head. Jon was engaged to an exciting, beautiful woman. His future was on course. At this point in his life, he didn't need to start obsessing over possibilities.

****

When Jon finished telling the tale, carefully omitting the content of the note and how it made him feel, he looked to the backseat for Suzanne's reaction. Her eyes were closed, and her head tipped to one side.

"Good job, Jonny boy," Travis said softly. "Lulled her right to sleep with your riveting remembrances. She needs the rest, so maybe you can tell the story again later."

Jon chuckled. Fine by him that Suzanne hadn't heard the whole thing. It was an embarrassment to his manhood. But more than that, each time he thought of the fishing expedition, he wondered what happened to the bottle and note. What if he had stuck the note in his pocket, and emailed the woman? He was surprised, after what he'd been through with Andrea, that he was even a tiny bit romantic.

As the only one of the college friends still single, he had the image of bachelor-for-life. The guys and their wives had been working on him in the last couple of years, trying to set him up. If he went to visit their homes, they'd have a dinner party planned, with an extra woman, single, smart, and beautiful. Without exception, he enjoyed their company, and just as universally, he'd been glad to say good-bye when they parted ways.

Two women, for wildly different reasons, had helped Jon realize he was a bad risk when it came to relationships—his ex-fiancée Andrea and Emily Standish's friend Kim.

Chapter Three

KIM'S SUITCASE STOOD inside the door of David and Emily's house. Emily had insisted on picking her up, so Kim's car could be in the garage of her duplex out of the weather while she was gone. Emily would check on Handsome, Kim's cat, every day and even said she didn't mind cleaning out the litter pan. Emily was a true friend in every possible way.

Kim sat on the couch, reading a picture book to Isabel. Kim was trying to do voices for the characters, and when she hit on a good one, Isabel giggled.

"Are you sure you don't want me to help in the kitchen, Emily?"

"You are helping, my dear. And doing a lovely job with the rabbits' voices. David should be here any minute. He'd better be, or Travis, Suzanne..." She turned away, toward the stove. "They may get here before he's back. I hope not."

"Hmm. I'm getting a diaper-change vibe, Emily. Want me to take care of it?"

Emily stopped what she was doing. "That's okay. I will." She came around the end of the bar and picked up her daughter. "So, maybe you could make sure nothing burns?" She and Isabel made their way to the bedroom and the changing table.

Chuckling, Kim stood and stretched and went into the galley kitchen. She checked the pots, peeked into the oven. Everything looked and smelled delicious. Having a big brunch felt like she was truly on vacation.

Emily's phone, sitting on the bar between kitchen and living area, sounded an alert. Without thinking, Kim automatically looked at it. It was a text from David. He always had some task to do on the family Christmas tree farm when he was home on weekends from his working travels.

tsj- ten mins. ill be there

Well, that was a bit cryptic. Since the food was fine, Kim decided to set the table. Emily had laid out the plates, glasses, and cloth napkins on the countertop. Kim picked them up, went to the table, and started to lay the places. Her hands stopped when she realized there were six of each, plus plastic ones for Isabel.

Her stomach sank. She thought back to David's hurried text. T was Travis, and S was Suzanne. *Who is J?* She was afraid she knew. And if she was right, she would be back home with her suitcase very soon. No way would she let herself get stuck in a car with Jon Whitfield.

No wonder Emily had offered to take care of Kim's neurotic cat, and said she didn't mind cleaning out the litter box. Kim was being set up.

****

The sedan crested the last emerald-green hill and laid below them was the little town of Serendipity. The castle-like limestone courthouse, majestically located in the center of the town square, could be seen even from here, a couple of miles away.

Travis slowed to the posted speed limit of forty, then thirty miles an hour, and when they approached the square, traffic was at a crawl.

Jon saw it all happen in slow motion, which it almost was. Travis stopped to let someone pull out of a diagonal parking space in front of one of the shops on the square. There was nothing he could do about it, but in his side mirror Jon watched the pickup truck run right into the rear of Travis's car. They were jolted, and the crunch of steel on steel set his teeth on edge

People from the sidewalk were at the car immediately. David's sister, Carla, who had a shop right there, talked to Suzanne, called Emily, then 911. An ambulance came. Soon Suzanne and Travis were on their way to Serendipity Hospital, and Carla drove Jon to join them. The whole thing was surreal. An eternity later, everyone was pronounced fine, though the ER doctor cautioned Suzanne to find a quiet place to get extra rest. Not the hospital, thank goodness. None of them wanted that.

****

Seven people sat at David and Emily's table with what would have been a beautiful meal if not for the wreck. The overcooked food and Kim Rose's sullen expression didn't help Jon's appetite. Little Isabel chattered almost constantly, as if trying to make up for the adults' mood.

Jon speared a sausage link. "The truck driver was looking down, and so was the girl with him. I saw it; they were probably texting. The police said they would check on that. It's the same in Tennessee. I've seen drivers with their phones in hand, speeding down the interstate."

Travis looked miserable. He seemed to blame himself. "The question is, now what? The meal is great, Emily, and we meant to hang out for a while and visit you guys, but we're behind schedule what with the accident and the trip to the hospital. I'm thankful the ER doc put my mind at ease about Suzanne." His wife was sitting next to him, and he slid an arm around her shoulders. "But we need to get going if we're still going to make the whole conference. From here we have at least an eleven-hour drive. Probably should have built an extra day in, but we didn't."

Emily stood and refilled everyone's coffee mugs. "Suzanne could stay here. Isabel and I would be glad to have her."

Suzanne held up a hand. "You're so sweet, Emily. But I feel fine, and I've been looking forward to this trip ever since Travis mentioned it. Plus, Kim is a nurse, so if I have any problems, she'll be right there. She and I have plans for when the guys are busy. Right, Kim?"

Kim's smile was halfhearted. She sagged into her chair, shot a brief glare at Jon.

Suzanne continued, hand on her tummy, "Travis and I are looking so forward to welcoming little Elliott into the world. But we're realistic; life will be forever changed once he's born. So I'm racking up lots of memories of life before kids."

Emily cleared her throat. "Kim, you've met Jon before, right? I'm sorry. In all the craziness that happened today, it just occurred to me that I didn't make introductions."

Kim nodded, looking directly into Jon's eyes for the first time. "Yes, we've met. You and your fiancée were here for the wedding."

"*Ex*-fiancée." He didn't expound on that. The state of his love-life was none of her business, and he'd told his friends what had happened with Andrea.

Jon could tell that Kim had been as unaware of his being on this trip as he had about her planning to come along to hang out with Suzanne. No wonder Travis and his wife had let some sentences trail off while finalizing plans and on the drive up. They'd probably been about to mention the fourth member of their traveling circus.

They knew if they had mentioned Kim, Jon would have reneged. Not because they had any idea of how she had behaved toward him, but because they knew that, post-Andrea, Jon was now relationship-resistant.

Jon and Travis could have flown, met at the conference, and avoided all this. If they had, Suzanne would be safe at home and Kim would be nowhere near him. But he had to deal with the current situation. He would not bail on his friends. If Suzanne was determined to make the trip, having a nurse along was a plus, no matter how awkward it was for him. He cleared his throat. "We'll need a rental car."

David shook his head, rose from the table, went to the door that led to the garage, and took a set of keys off a hook. He returned and handed them to Jon. "Take the Suburban."

Emily groaned softly.

David kissed the top of her head before reclaiming his seat. "Okay. Warning. It's a mess inside. But the oil was changed last week, and it's a good ride. Plenty of room for your stuff in the back, and space for everyone to be comfortable."

"That's so kind, David," Suzanne said. "But we could rent a car or a small SUV."

David, Emily, and Kim all shook their heads.

"Afraid not," David said. "We haven't had a car rental lot in town for a few years now. Please take the Suburban. Of course, you'll be out some money feeding my beloved gas hog." He took out his wallet and produced a gas card.

Jon pushed the card away but set the keys on the table. "Driving a Suburban will involve a learning curve, I'm sure. Travis's sedan has been interesting compared to my Corvette. But any option is better than none. We'll deal with feeding the gas hog. Thanks, D."

Kim held her hand out toward Jon. "If you're worried about the curve, let me drive the first shift. I have experience with larger vehicles."

Travis wasn't ready to get behind a wheel. He still seemed a bit shaken from today's crunch on the square, and Jon knew he would look like a jerk if he refused Kim's offer, so he handed her the keys. He ignored the slight shock of static when their hands touched, a weird thing for this time of year.

He had to admit, for Suzanne's sake, it was a good idea to have Kim along. For Travis, too, since the guy had become a Class A worrier. Jon would just get through the trip as well as possible, keeping interaction with Kim to a minimum. He knew from previous experience that he could expect to have his head bitten off if he talked to the woman. When they arrived at the conference, Jon would have no reason to be around her. Then, when the conference was over, he'd manage to endure the ride home. It wasn't an ideal plan, but seemed the only one available.

Not wanting to get further behind schedule, they went into action right after the meal. With Suzanne repeatedly assuring everyone how fine she felt, they piled their bags into the Suburban. The cargo area was big enough that Jon didn't have to dump out the box or two of David's stuff that looked like they'd been there for a decade. No reason to point a finger at David's lifelong reputation of being a slob, when the guy was letting them put loads of extra miles on his vehicle.

Kim dug in her massive handbag and handed David a set of keys. "Drive my Smart car. Enjoy the mobility. Do *no*t fill it with clutter." She hugged him, Emily, and gave Isabel a noisy kiss.

So she wouldn't be by the air bag, Suzanne had opted to sit in the back seat, "even though I'd love to sit up front and chat with you, Kim." Everyone said brief goodbyes, and they were on their way. David's friend had an auto repair shop and promised to have the wrecked car repaired by the time they returned.

Jon gritted his teeth to be stuck riding shotgun. He was discontented with David's preprogrammed radio stations and adjusted the temperature until everybody told him to stop fidgeting. What was he supposed to do sitting here next to this woman who hated his guts? He wished for an atlas or a book of any sort. Maybe he could pretend to fall asleep and nap all the way to the conference.

****

A couple of hours later, at Suzanne's request, Kim pulled into a rest stop. She preferred her tiny car but was comfortable with the big vehicle. She'd spent many day trips behind the wheel of a van back when she worked at the rehab facility in New Albany.

Travis and Jon walked ahead, toward the restroom building. Suzanne said in a low voice, "I'm almost glad that truck rear-ended us. Otherwise, I can imagine Jon deciding to fly the remainder of the way to the conference venue instead of going with us. I just don't know what's wrong with him."

"Suzanne, if not for that pickup truck, I would have stayed home, you know. I really wish you and Travis and David and Emily hadn't set me up this way."

"It's for your own good, honey. You say you're a romantic. I've heard you. Well, you and Jon are *romantically* perfect for each other."

"Nothing of the kind. He looks at me like I'm the devil, and I—I have a bad feeling about him."

Suzanne was astonished. "But you barely know him."

Kim shrugged. "Doesn't matter. I'll deal with the situation, but please forget any ideas about Jon and me falling in love with each other because you tricked us into a road trip. That's a bit high school, isn't it?"

Suzanne giggled. "Emily and I had a good time planning it. You wanted a vacation, Travis had the conference. And, oh yeah, I wanted to make memories and not be left at home. If I was back there right now, I'd be cleaning house and ironing for my work week, but instead I'm on vacation, having an adventure."

The woman's enthusiasm was hard to resist. Kim told herself she'd be upbeat and not let Jon's presence spoil the vacation she'd been looking forward to.

Suzanne interrupted her musings. "Anyone can see you're special, Kim. So caring and gentle.

Super competent. Emily's told me stories of how you go out of your way to help patients and their families. The first time we met you, at their wedding in Serendipity, Travis and I both felt as if we'd known you for years. We're so happy together and want to see others in a loving relationship too. Thus...matchmaking." Suzanne winked and went ahead into the restroom, leaving Kim in the outer area by the maps and flyers.

Living in Serendipity was bad enough with everyone knowing everyone else's business or making it up. Matchmaking hadn't been a problem until now, and it was a big one. She had a love/hate relationship with Jon Whitfield, whom she hardly knew. She would be in his presence for so many hours while they were on the road that she knew something was going to blow. She just didn't know if that something was Jon—or her.

Chapter Four

ALL ALONE IN a vehicle full of people, Jon scrolled through stuff on his phone without seeing it, trying to block out any other thoughts. What was it with Kim—always flashing megawatt smiles at whoever was around, but she looked daggers at Jon each time their eyes met? It wasn't that he wanted her attention, but the way she behaved, he knew she was hiding something. Jon knew a thing or two about women who were expert at pretense.

Jon glanced over at her for a couple of seconds. She had her eyes on the road, unaware of him, which was ideal. To look at her wide eyes and flawless skin, it'd be easy to think she was sweet and innocent. But he'd bet money that she was no more innocent than Andrea had been. Why was he the only one who was aware of this dichotomy in Kim's behavior?

This conference could make all the difference to Jon's future. Having the pretty, vivacious Kim next to him was a distraction, in spite of the way she treated him, at a time when he needed to be on top of his game. But once they reached their destination, she'd be off his radar. He'd be concentrating on business and some high-powered networking.

Suzanne planned to accompany Travis to the first evening meet-and-greet. Jon hoped his friends didn't expect him to squire Kim to the event. Conference attendees had been encouraged to bring a significant other, but Jon didn't mind attending stag. Better stag than having a tramp on his arm, like he'd had the first time he met Kim.

****

Jon remembered the weekend of David and Emily's wedding—a time that should have been joyful but turned out to be one of Jon's worst. He and Andrea had landed at the Louisville airport and were on their way to pick up their rental car, when the fight that had been brewing all day finally came to a head. It wasn't their first major disagreement, by any means, but it was the worst—a culmination of his distaste for her constant flirting with other men. At a loss to understand her behavior, Jon lashed out, accused her of cheating on him. To his shock and surprise, she admitted it, almost proudly.

Turned out, she was doing it with the guy he was competing with for an important promotion.

Evidently, no matter which of them got the pay raise and corner office, Andrea intended to benefit.

Andrea, having ended the charade, turned cold and hateful. She was a smart woman, a VP in a marketing firm, and knew how and when to use the connections she had so skillfully built. Jon guessed—correctly, it turned out—that splitting with Andrea would mean he didn't get the promotion.

After squabbling in a corner of the airport common area, they looked into an early flight back for her, but everything was booked. Andrea didn't seem concerned and refused to be dropped off at a Louisville hotel until the return flight.

"You'll just have to take me to the wedding," she said. "Everyone is expecting me, right? You wouldn't want to have to explain my absence and accidentally upstage your friend's big day."

The drive from Louisville to David's hometown seemed to go on forever. At least, there was an extra room at the hotel at the edge of Serendipity. Jon's knees nearly buckled with relief when the desk clerk verified they had the space. "It's on the second floor though," she said, a question in her eyes. "And yours is on the first. It's late, and everyone else is checked in, or else I'd try—"

"Perfect," Andrea spat out. "I'll take the first floor room. At least that puts me near that pitiful little pool."

But the pool wasn't going to keep her from attending the wedding. He knew she didn't want to go any more than he wanted her there. He'd had to beg to get her to come, not wanting his friends to think something was wrong with their relationship. He'd been fooling himself, and probably the guys knew that. They'd met Andrea at Ryan's wedding the year before. She'd been at her most attractive, meaning she was in a good mood, at which time she was like a magnet to metal filings.

How he wished she would stay at the hotel. He could make an excuse for her, say she was sick.

"I'm not staying in a hotel room in the middle of Nowhere, USA, for the whole weekend with nothing to do. Come on, Jon. One last time to show me off."

He wouldn't allow himself to lose his temper with her again, so they sat together in a pew during the service and walked together down the stairs to the reception. Strangers stared at the radiant blond beauty next to him with her perfect hair, smile, and makeup. Her dress was too extravagant, but that was intentional. Andrea always needed to be the center of attention.

Once they were in the cluster of guests at the reception, Jon was relieved when she wandered away. He'd never again worry about her flirtatiousness. Let the world beware.

Although the event itself was simple, the crowd was large. It seemed the whole town was in attendance. Jon's mood was lifted by being surrounded by so many smiling people, and David was glowing almost as much as his bride. He had seemed happily settled in his bachelor life, and all the guys had been blindsided when he announced his engagement to a local girl he'd never mentioned before.

Emily was several years younger but so self-assured, so kind. During the wedding, and especially at the reception, her dark-haired bridesmaid caught Jon's attention. Pretty girl with expressive eyes and an infectious enthusiasm that affected everyone in the room.

The bride appeared at Jon's side doing a pass through the crowd, while David did the same on the other side of the room. Emily linked her arm through Jon's and drew him over to where her bridesmaid stood. "So, have the two of you met? Kim, this is David's good friend, Jon. And Jon, my fabulous pal, Kim Rose."

If Andrea was looking at him right now, Jon wasn't sure she'd have more venom in her eyes than this girl, Kim. She seemed to instantly dislike him.

Yet during the wedding and a few minutes later at the reception when he saw her from a distance, she'd been happy and upbeat. Was he wearing a *Hate Me* sign on his back?

Jon said something inane, smiling and waiting for Kim to shake his hand, but she didn't offer.

She appeared ready to dash off somewhere—anywhere. But Emily still had her arms linked through each of theirs. She drew them to the end of the room, where long tables were laden with homemade casseroles of every description instead of a catered buffet.

"Why don't the two of you grab some dinner and sit together, so you can get to know each other? We're not doing the traditional separate table for the wedding party. I don't even know where David and I will end up eating." Her radiance showed she couldn't have cared less about details like seating plans. She was thrilled to be married to the man she loved.

David was lucky to have Emily. She was fun, and caring—nothing like Andrea.

Replying to Emily, Kim's voice was low. "Not sure why you're pushing the two of us together. I mean, Jon has a date." She looked around for Andrea.

The bride laughed. "We just want everybody to be as happy as we are."

Jon knew when he was being cornered. None of his friends liked Andrea. They'd tried to warn him away, perhaps seeing her for what she was. But this was the worst possible time to endure an episode of matchmaking.

They went through the food line, but at the end, he mumbled an excuse about needing to talk to Ryan and Dustin. He made his escape without, he hoped, looking desperate to do so. He couldn't endure Kim's glares any longer.

It wasn't long before David clapped him on the shoulder. "How's our last single friend holding up? Is the wedding and reception as much of a turnoff to you as they always were to me, before Emily?"

Jon couldn't help the grin, feeling a bit relieved. "I'm glad you can understand, David. I'm really happy for you, of course."

David nodded. "But you wish you were home, wearing sweats and watching a game on TV. Yep. But one of these days, Jon, you'll find the woman who makes weddings and receptions bearable. Even your own." He looked around then, as Kim had done earlier. "Where is the amazing Andrea, anyway? You haven't come to your senses about her, have you?"

Jon shook his head. "Long, ugly story, and not one you need to hear on your wedding day, my friend."

A melodic laugh caught Jon's ear and he saw Kim across the room, talking with David's sisters and a couple of other women. He glimpsed Andrea, making the most of every interaction with a male as she worked her way through the crowd toward the drinks table.

David was still talking, the DJ was playing Norah Jones's *Come Away with Me*, and a voice in Jon's head whispered that Kim was the woman for him.

Which was nuts given her immediate dislike of him, the fact that Andrea would be on a rampage when they got out of here, and the unlikelihood of Jon and Kim ever seeing each other again after tonight.

For the remainder of the reception, Jon managed to avoid awkward moments. The women had started the DJ on a line-dancing jag, so Jon stood with his buddies in a corner of the fellowship hall, retelling old stories from college days. With that he was comfortable again.

But those good old days were further and further in the past. Not just because of the passage of time, but also because of the addition of wives and probably children in the near future. That was not the life for Jon though. He much preferred casual relationships with women, the kind that wouldn't complicate his world. He tried to remember why he'd let himself slip into this mess with Andrea, not just exclusive dating but becoming engaged. But he couldn't come up with anything. He must have been out of his mind.

Probably just another example of going with the flow, which he'd done too often in his personal life. Going with the flow, like a bottle on the ocean, being carried along with the flotsam of life until, in a random and meaningless trick of current, its journey ended. There was nothing magical about it.

Jon didn't believe in magic—or in love.

Chapter Five

THE ROLLING HILLS of Southern Indiana were behind them, and here on the plains, flat as an exam room table, Kim could see for miles in all directions. A storm was on its way. The sky was dreary now, but in the west, a bank of dark, roiling clouds threatened. The uninhibited view was unsettling, partly because the SUV and its occupants appeared even more exposed to whatever might come along. There were plenty of other vehicles, from semis and giant RVs, down to an occasional motorcycle. She wondered about those. Where would the cyclists seek shelter when the storm hit? Below an overpass in the filth, noise, and spray as other traffic sped past? Or were they nearly home?

Kim was glad the SUV was heavy. Maybe its weight wouldn't make it too difficult to stay in their lane when the winds hit. She glanced quickly again toward the west, her hands tightening on the steering wheel. She wouldn't freak out. It was just a thunderstorm.

She had been driving home from work a few years ago when tornado sirens started wailing, the weather alert on her phone went off, and the familiar scenery around her spun out of control in the whipping winds and onslaught of heavy rain. *A few minutes more and I'll be home.* But a car stalled out at the top of an interstate exit two miles from her apartment. The handful of vehicles and their occupants stuck behind that vehicle were trapped. There was no cover nearby to run to.

Kim had prayed hard, tried to remember how to meditate, and attempted to avoid panic. She automatically grabbed the phone to call her mom, and was met with the memories of her funeral a few days earlier.

Kim had survived, of course. They were lucky because the tornado didn't go through that area. Others, however, were not so fortunate.

And today she was responsible for everyone in the vehicle. Travis and Suzanne asleep in the backseat, and Jon.

Would it be wise to pull off and let the storm pass? She didn't know how long that might take. They were already behind schedule, and the long day in the SUV seemed unbearable. Her hands, arms, and back were sore from driving. She hazarded a look at Jon, who sat, relaxed, scrolling on his phone. He had offered to spell her at the wheel when they stopped at the rest area, and now she wished she'd agreed. He would be used to the Suburban by now and might feel confident despite the storm. Or, at least, she would be less tired now, if he had driven for a while.

But no. She had shut him down when he offered, and now she was reaping her reward. She'd learned self-sufficiency the hard way, thrown into a nightmare when her mother became ill, and even more so when she died. Later when Kim herself was diagnosed, the only person in the world she thought she could depend on failed her completely. She hadn't given up, but the treatments' side effects would have been easier to bear if she'd had a companion to help her through. Someone to make some soup or go out at midnight to buy whatever food or drink her sick, exhausted body craved, just so she could manage to ingest some calories to continue to fight.

But she'd had none of those. She was lucky that one of the families on the ground floor of her apartment building included a teenage boy, proud of his football muscles and glad to make a few bucks by carrying groceries up the staircase for the bald, sick lady.

Another quick glance left. It wouldn't be long now.

"Want to take the next exit, Kim?"

The soft, unexpected question from Jon startled her from her thoughts.

He shifted, turning his body toward hers a bit, as if to show her something on his phone. "Looks like there's a mall just off the interstate. Maybe we could park on the east side of a building and get some protection from the wind. From what my weather app says, it's a fast-moving storm. We can't outrun it, but if we wait here a little while, we should drive out of the worst of it before long." He set his phone on the console. "And if you want, I'll take a turn at driving."

If he'd read her thoughts, he couldn't have said anything more welcome.

She summoned a calm tone. "Good idea to pull off, at least for a little while. If you're willing to try driving this monster, I'd be glad for a break. You'll have your hands full, though. You know the warnings about high profile vehicles and crosswinds."

"Got it. But did you know I drive a Corvette? Have you ever driven one in a storm? Not the most reassuring experience. It's a bit prone to hydroplaning, and water pooled on the road really looks ominous when you're sitting just a few inches above it."

Kim chuckled, felt immediately better because of it. She turned on her signal and left the interstate. In a few minutes, she had parked near the east side of a mall store and shut off the engine.

Suzanne and Travis stirred. Sitting up straight and wiping tired eyes, Suzanne met Kim's in the rearview mirror. Kim turned with her patented Smile of Reassurance firmly in place. She'd used it thousands of times on patients.

"Hey. Sorry to disturb you guys. A storm's about to hit and we decided to wait here a few minutes. And Jon is going to drive for a while when we start again." She took a breath, noticed her pulse had slowed since parking. She smiled again and cast about for anything to say. "And while we're here, is there anything you need?" She jerked a thumb toward the building.

Suzanne's eyes followed her gesture, and she laughed. "I'm okay for now, but if you want to shop, go for it."

Jon chuckled too, covering his mouth with a hand. His eyes crinkled in humor. Kim's Smile of Reassurance slid when she realized they were at the entrance of a lingerie store. Her face was flaming. "Guess I should pay better attention to where I shelter from a storm. Too bad there's not a bookstore on this side."

Jon's humor disappeared. "You don't have to do the innocent act for us, Kim. Now, let's switch seats before the rain hits."

****

Jon strode around the SUV and had his hand on the door handle when Kim finally opened it. She shot him a hateful look—hardly the thanks he expected for offering to drive despite this ugly change in weather. He took a step back, letting Kim slide out of the seat and pass him without getting too close. His patience with her innate dislike of him had grown thin, and he'd like to tell her to stop being such a witch. But he didn't want to upset his friends. They seemed to view her as their own personal angel of mercy.

He could handle it. This trip wouldn't last forever, though it seemed it already had. Kim's prickly reaction to his lingerie store comment was hilarious. She sure played the innocent part well.

When she was settled in the passenger seat, he asked, "Let me guess. In your spare time, you're active in the local community theater scene." Had to be, since she was so good at facade.

She looked genuinely perplexed. "No. Why would you think so?"

Her Little Miss Priss act was almost convincing. Part of Jon wanted to believe it. Then he made the mistake of noticing the way the wind had messed with her hair. The portion collected in a clasp at her nape was always messy, but his hand ached to tuck a wayward strand behind her ear.

Crazy. The woman was making him crazy.

A couple of teenage girls dashed from their car to the lingerie store, just as the torrents of rain began. The girls screamed and laughed and were soaked to the skin in a moment, their expensive looking handbags and shoes probably ruined.

Jon checked the rearview. "Kids," he said. "Were we ever that stupid, Travis? To run out in a downpour?"

Travis was staring out the window on his side. "We did plenty of things that stupid, Jon. Though to be honest, I don't remember a women's underwear shop in any of our escapades. Wouldn't have been a bad thing. Might be a stop to add to our next trip."

"Before or after the trout fishing?"

Travis unbuckled his seat belt and scooted next to Suzanne, taking her hand into his. "Before, I'm guessing. By the time we've roughed it for a few days, they probably wouldn't let us into the store."

Kim was smiling, looked like she was calming down. Jon wished she'd relax around him instead of being nice one minute then when he was involved, get all prickly again.

Rain blasted, coming at them horizontally, and winds buffeted the vehicle. Jon wondered if they should have gone indoors. With the windows up tight and the air conditioner off, the small space grew warm and close. Kim's light floral perfume called to him, and with determination, he pulled out his phone to check emails and see what was blowing up at work right now.

Chapter Six

TRAVIS WAS DRIVING when they pulled into the impressive hotel complex shortly before midnight. "Is this the door we want, Jon?"

Jon had his ever-present phone out, having reviewed their signup materials and a layout of the place. "Yep, this is us. At least this time of night, we won't be standing in line at the hotel desk to get our rooms."

That was the only positive thing about arriving so late. When Kim found herself in her beautifully appointed room, she was so exhausted, she almost wondered how she'd gotten there. The wreck, the storm, a couple of forgettable fast food meals and gas station stops, plus some rest areas on the way had made the miserably long day almost unbearable. But they had arrived, safely.

Once they checked in, Jon said a quick good night and dashed off with his bags to catch up on work emails, he said. She rode up in the elevator with Travis and Suzanne. They offered to walk her to her door.

"No thanks, I'm fine. Just ready to collapse onto a comfortable bed. I'll see you both tomorrow."

She smiled tiredly at them both and pulled her rolling bag down the hallway, found her door, and unlocking it, leaned against the door frame with great relief.

Alone, finally. She was used to being on her own a lot since her mother died and her boyfriend disappeared. The road trip had been exhausting on so many levels—not a vacation at all. Now, maybe relaxation and rejuvenation could begin.

She pulled out her sleep T, took a shower, then crawled into bed.

****

When Kim woke up, bright light was peeking at the edges of the curtains. When her eyes were able to focus on the bedside clock, she was shocked to see it was after nine. She got up, dug in her bag for her phone.

A text from Emily popped up, asking how everything was and accompanied by a video of Handsome sitting on the back of Kim's sofa, switching his tail and looking ticked off.

At least everything at home was normal. Kim sent a text back with a photo of her hotel room. *Slept great. Vacation has begun. Thx to you, kisses to Isabel, and hi to Handsome.*

She set down the phone and started to unpack. She'd asked Suzanne to let her know when she was up and wanted to have breakfast. At this rate, maybe they'd meet for lunch instead, not that it mattered.

She was hanging her black dress in the closet when a notification sounded. A text from Suzanne. *Hi. You up? I'm ravenous!*

Twenty minutes later, they met in the lobby.

"Travis slept later than he meant to. I hope they're in time for the first session," Suzanne said. "Jon hates to arrive late for anything. He's a little OCD."

Kim stopped outside the hotel restaurant, looked at the posted menu. "There's a surprise."

"Kim, I thought maybe you two would start to like each other a little when you spent some time together, but that's not happening yet. Looks like our little matchmaking project is painful for the two of you. I'm sorry. I really do apologize."

The maître d' showed them to a booth. Kim slid in and Suzanne struggled a bit to do the same. *Note to self. Ask for a table next time.* "It's okay, Suzanne. Let's not worry about it. We're finally here after the road trip from Heck, and you and I can have some fun seeing the sights, as planned.

Their waiter appeared, and they both ordered coffee. "I have to get decaf," Suzanne pouted. "Because of Elliott. But I'm going to pretend it's high-test."

When they'd both ordered their meals, Suzanne shook her head, frowning. "I still feel bad. In the evening when Travis and I are having dinner, trying out the smart restaurants in town, going dancing—slowly of course—you'll be all by yourself. That stinks."

Kim patted her handbag where her e-reader was. "No worries. I've downloaded plenty of books. Remember, I always expected you and Travis to want time alone. This trip is part babymoon for you, after all. I'm just fine being on my own."

Yet at this moment, saying that, she felt anything but fine. The longer she was around Jon, the more she wondered if she had judged him too harshly.

Suzanne picked up her phone. "I got a text from Travis. He and Jon barely made it to the keynote speech, but they're set now." She slid the phone into her bag. "That's a relief. You and I have the day to ourselves." She sighed. "Finally, the relaxation portion of this trip."

Kim looked into her friend's eyes, expecting signs of exhaustion. "You sure you're up for it?"

Suzanne, having made quick work of breakfast, hitched her bag onto her shoulder. "Honey, I've slept off and on for the last two days, riding in the back of a car. I'm raring to go."

After breakfast, they went to the hotel concierge desk and gathered flyers. They'd both done online research and made some general plans from that when talking about the trip.

The first sites they visited were places made famous by the *Mary Tyler Moore Show*. They each had their photo taken near the statue of Mary throwing her tam into the air in exuberant celebration.

Suzanne immediately texted a photo. "My mom is going to be so excited. This was one of her favorite shows of all time. I bought her the DVD collection a couple years ago for Christmas."

Kim was silent. Her mother would have loved seeing photos of these places too and reminiscing about episodes of the groundbreaking TV series centered on a single career woman. But cancer had stolen Kim's mother from her. Later, it tried to take Kim herself.

She and Suzanne wandered through a variety of sites, taking silly selfies, reading bits of history. Eventually they were lured by their senses of smell to the sidewalk dining area of an Indian restaurant.

When their glasses of water arrived, Suzanne took a long drink. "I've wanted to check Minnesota off my list of states to visit, so when this conference popped up for Travis's work, it seemed perfect."

Kim sighed. "Not quite perfect with Jon and me along."

Suzanne winked. "We love you both, even if you don't love each other."

Kim enjoyed travel but wasn't keen to do it on her own. If not for Suzanne's invitation, she might never have visited this beautiful city. If not for the Romantic Hearts Book Club, she wouldn't have visited Enchanted Island where she pitched her message in a bottle into the Caribbean.

Her eyes drifted to a nearby table where a couple had ordered wine to go with their lunch. Where was her message in a bottle? Still floating on the sea somewhere? Several book club members had reported their bottles were found in unusual locations. Maybe Kim's had been carried to the other end of the world on a series of tides. Maybe no one would ever find it, or if they did, wouldn't take the time to email her. But she'd made it clear in her note that she didn't expect anything from the exercise, hadn't she?

Kim knew life didn't bring many unexpected happy surprises. Her scholarship to nursing school had been one, but she'd applied for that, worked hard to be worthy of the honor. Working hard, trying to be worthy hadn't done much good in the rest of her life though.

It hadn't kept her mother alive.

It hadn't kept Kim from being diagnosed and having to undergo treatment for breast cancer.

And it hadn't kept her boyfriend, Sean, from turning out to be a loser. The day she explained her diagnosis and treatment plan to him, he packed his belongings and moved out.

That's what happened when you put trust in the wrong person. Kim would never do that again.

****

After lunch and browsing a few stores, Kim could see Suzanne's energy flagging. They got fruit smoothies and found a taxi for the ride back to the hotel. Disembarking at the front of the building, they were greeted by a doorman who held the door for them.

They sank onto chaise lounges on a patio, where they could enjoy fresh air and the warm afternoon without any exertion.

Suzanne sighed in delight. "Goodness, I'll have to be careful not to get used to this life. Going back home to my world could be a letdown."

But Suzanne would be returning to a home with a loving husband and a baby on the way. Kim didn't envy Suzanne's happiness—she was glad for her. She felt the same about Emily. Kim was determined to be satisfied with what life had given her and what she'd been able to do with that. A career, good friends... She'd written something about that in the note she'd slid into a bottle and sent into the unknown, hadn't she? Maybe someone had found it and thought she didn't really want a man in her life.

Kim did want a man. But she was willing to wait for the right man this time, to be cautious instead of falling head over heels in love the first time she set eyes on a guy. That's how it had been with Sean, and it had ended in utter disaster at one of the lowest points of her life. Message-in-a-bottle or no, she was determined to wait for the real thing this time. No matter how long it took.

Sean's handsome face had haunted her dreams, especially shortly after he deserted her. She knew she'd never see him again, so when she looked into the crowd after Emily's wedding and saw him looking across the room at her, her heart skipped a beat. *How dare he show up here on this happy day?*

But it hadn't been Sean. Some cruel twist of fate resulted in David Standish having a friend from college who looked enough like Sean, whom David and Emily had never met, to be his twin. Jon Whitfield. Even though she knew Sean had no brothers, and she knew it made no sense to immediately dislike David's friend, she couldn't help herself.

The fact that Jon paid no attention to his fiancée during the reception convinced her there was a similarity between his personality and Sean's.

When she looked at Jon, she saw the pain of her past that wasn't as well healed as she'd thought.

She didn't have nightmares about Sean anymore. She had made her peace with that situation—even managed, on good days, to feel sorry for the handsome man who seemed to lack empathy. What would it be like to go through life not feeling for people who were suffering? Sean said she took other people's problems too personally, but Kim didn't know how to keep herself from caring. And she didn't want to try.

Caring made her a good nurse and also made the job super hard when patients weren't able to recover fully or when they died. Kim went through a semblance of the family's grief with them. That was who she was, why she and Emily had become such close friends, and part of the reason for this trip. She had to get away sometimes, because the way she did her job, some days and nights she felt like she was riding an emotional roller coaster. Time away was required, so she could return to the hospital floor rested, rejuvenated, and ready to do her best for each patient.

But to travel without friends made her feel hopelessly alone. She had no blood family anymore, but thanks to Emily and her connections, she was building another kind of family. She didn't expect it, but the friendships forged through the online book club were strong and loving. The island vacation to see everyone in person was wonderful, and Kim hoped they could get together again sometime. But if they did, would Kim be the only one who still hadn't found love?

It was a depressing thought and one she wouldn't allow. She sank further into the chair and released her hair from its clasp and let it blow in the wind. She was on vacation in a lovely spot and wouldn't allow anything to ruin it for her.

Not the past and not the presence of Jon Whitfield.

Chapter Seven

A BURST OF conversation awakened Kim. She had fallen asleep in the deck chair next to Suzanne's. The deck was now full of people with nametags hanging around their necks by lime green lanyards.

Travis squatted next to Suzanne, holding her hand. Jon lurked, brooding, behind him. Travis's eyes sparked. "So, it's opening night festivities in a couple of hours, Kim. I was just telling Suzanne that a few people weren't able to attend at the last minute. We grabbed you a ticket. Isn't that great?"

"Oh. Well, sure, but I..."

Jon perked up, looking glad she was trying to talk her way out of it.

Kim straightened in the chair. "Thanks, guys, but I've got an appointment with a good book."

Suzanne laughed. "Come on, Kim. We'll have more fun if you're there. You said you brought your little black dress, just in case. So you can't beg off for not having anything to wear."

Kim sat up straighter, the better to hold a firm line. "I have the dress and heels, but not the energy. You'll all have a good time, and I will get rested up for tomorrow's sightseeing." She shot a look to Suzanne that she hoped would be respected. *Give me an easy out here, please.*

Suzanne's smile dimmed, registering the fact that Kim's decision wouldn't change. "Well, okay. We'll miss you. I'll be in my maternity not-so-little black dress, which isn't as cute as its predecessor. But I'm good with that. I like looking pregnant."

Travis leaned in and gave Suzanne a long, thorough kiss. "Pregnant and gorgeous."

Jon looked away, and Kim felt her face heat. There wasn't anything inappropriate about their behavior, yet the moment was intimate. When the kiss ended, she thanked them again for the invitation and excused herself, retreating to her beautiful, solitary hotel room.

****

Kim's window was open so she could enjoy the soft evening breeze. She could hear the gathering sound and energy of the welcome night event. The conference goers and their husbands, wives, and/or whatevers seemed to be a merry bunch. Work hard, play hard, perhaps. Kim smiled, glad that her presence helped make the event possible for Suzanne.

On their way downstairs, her friends stopped by Kim's room. Suzanne appeared refreshed after her nap. "We wish you could join us, Kim. The party would be more fun with you there. You light up a room, you know."

Kim shook her head, the hair brushing her shoulders bared by a ratty tank top she wore with flannel PJ bottoms. She wished for the clasp she'd left on the bathroom sink. "Thanks for that, but I won't be lighting up any rooms tonight. Instead of taking an extended nap as wiser women might have done, when I came upstairs I finished unpacking, read some, and did a bit of planning for our day tomorrow. Subject to your approval, of course. Tonight I'm staying in, and the two of you are going to have a fun evening being a couple. Forget I'm here, please. I'm not your guest, just a fellow traveler. I'm also not your mom, so I won't be doing a curfew check." She took Suzanne by the shoulders. "Go. Have fun. Hercule Poirot will provide me with all the excitement I need.

Suzanne and Travis started briefly before registering the name of Agatha Christie's famous mystery novel detective.

Travis took his wife's hand. "Understood, Kim. You and Hercule have a great evening."

"Oh, we will. Never a dull moment with him."

Before closing her door, she watched them go down the hall, hand in hand. Taking a deep breath, she was about to shut the door when the one across the hall opened. Jon stepped into the corridor, looking delicious in business-casual attire that didn't look like it came out of a suitcase, hair slightly damp from his shower. Kim took a quick sniff of air. Yum. He smelled good too.

Watch it, Kim. Don't fall for a handsome face again.

He hesitated when he saw her then closed the door behind him. "Well, this is a surprise. I heard voices out here but didn't realize..." He stopped, a strange look coming over his face. "Are you entertaining this evening?"

"Enterta— Oh, that was just Suzanne and Travis being sweet and asking me again to come along to the welcome night."

He nodded. "Travis said they hoped you would. I think they feel bad having fun and leaving you alone."

Was there a note of agreement in his voice? "As I told them, I'm glad to have an early night. I'm surprised you and Travis feel like partying. You didn't get any more sleep in the car than I did."

He shrugged, and she noticed he looked anything but energetic. "We're here for the continuing ed, but also for the networking. To skip any of it would be a mistake we might regret. A missed opportunity that won't come around again." He smiled tiredly, pulled his name badge out of a back pocket by its lanyard to reassure himself that he hadn't forgotten it, then replaced it. "You just never know how or when your future might take a turn, so you have to be ready. Enjoy your early night, Kim."

She closed the door softly, locked it, and settled into the comfy wing back chair by the window. She picked up her e-reader but didn't turn it on. She looked out her window at the skyline and thought about Jon. How amazing. Tonight the two of them had actually had an enjoyable conversation, their first, and he'd even allowed her a peek into his world. Instead of coming across as self-assured to the point of being obnoxious, he was perhaps not so different from Kim. Just doing his best for his career and preparing for change in case it came along. And, she had to admit, doing his best for Travis and Suzanne.

But there was still Jon's uncanny resemblance to her former boyfriend that colored every interaction she had with him. The moment she saw Jon at David and Emily's wedding, her heart had stopped, thinking her ex was there for some reason. She never wanted to see that man again. Handsome, smart, and funny, he'd turned out to be absolutely spineless, deserting her when he she thought he was the one person she could count on.

Yet, now she'd been in Jon Whitfield's presence during a road trip that had begun to seem endless, he seemed to the kind of man she could be interested in. Now that she knew him better, he didn't seem to be much like Sean at all. He watched out for Suzanne, had been concerned about Travis's reaction to being behind the wheel during the crunch on the Serendipity square. He paid attention to people in a way that not everyone did.

But Kim's life and Jon's were so different. She was happy working in a small town hospital, and getting to know the people in the community where she was trying to rebuild her life. Jon had a powerful position in a factory and was here to network with others, preparing to position himself for a move further up the proverbial ladder of success. He seemed to have little time for anything but work and an annual trip with his college buddies.

But when he smiled, he didn't look much like Sean anymore.

Chapter Eight

JON TRIED TO keep his mind on the networking opportunities of the welcome night, exchanging stories and business cards with the other participants. The background music of soft jazz, not loud or overpowering, was just enough to help ensure a relaxed atmosphere. The finger food was delicious, and the drinks flowed freely.

Had Kim eaten dinner? She looked exhausted and oh so huggable with her hair down, dressed for relaxing. What would she do if he showed up with one of the little plastic plates piled high with sandwiches and fruit and carrying a glass of wine? What would she do if he asked to come in and sit with her a while? Probably shut the door in his face and tell him to buzz off.

He brought his mind back to the room full of people. Suzanne seated on one of the high stools was smiling, looking beautiful. Travis stood next to her with a protective hand where her waist used to be. The road trip had been more adventure than intended, but Jon was glad he could help make it happen for them. Suzanne kept saying she was storing up memories for after the birth of baby

Elliott. When Jon first heard it, the idea seemed odd, but it made a lot of sense to intentionally step away from ordinary day-to-day life instead of treading the same path so long it became a rut.

That was one reason he was here, of course. To seek opportunities for the factory he managed. His people had the skill—generations of it in some cases. They just needed enough orders to fill so the employees had sufficient work hours to make a decent living. The industry landscape seemed to change daily, one company buying another and either changing everything, downsizing, or outsourcing. Stuff like that happened all the time. In fact, many of the men and women at the conference had personal horror stories of one sort or another.

Jon had been lucky so far—at least with his career. The biggest curveball life had thrown him was his disastrous relationship with Andrea. He'd taken a long time to wake up to the fact that she wasn't what she seemed. He wouldn't fall into that trap again.

He imagined Kim again. What was up with her? She seemed honest enough, but at the oddest times she would completely shift gears, changing from outgoing and fun to almost shutting down. He wasn't sure if he wanted to know what her past held, but if he could get more information, maybe he would understand what caused her mood swings. And what drew him to her.

If Andrea was his type, then Kim didn't really fit the mold. She wasn't runway model beautiful like Andrea. She didn't dress to impress or use much makeup that he could tell. Her hair was dark and thick, always trying to escape its clasp, instead of welded into a particular shape with hairspray. It was a welcome surprise to find a woman who was satisfied to be herself and let others like her, or not. Many of the people he interacted with in his profession worked hard to be what the customer, or the higher-ups, wanted them to be.

Jon had done plenty of that in his time, and if he was honest, he still did it. Attending this gathering, for instance, when he would have preferred a quiet night in like Kim or a few laps in the pool. But that wasn't his reason for being here. He might have a chance to relax when he got home. But this could be his only chance to get to know Kim. After this trip he probably would never see her again. And if he didn't act now, he would never understand this compulsion to be with her.

But what if she rebuffed him? He'd just have to deal with it if she did. At least, then, he'd know where he stood with her.

Jon looked at the mingling crowd and then gave himself a little shake. What the heck. Columbus took a chance. So could he.

Jon headed back to the buffet table. A couple of guys he'd met earlier in the day stopped to talk with him. Ball scores, politics, the weather. Conversation he could get anywhere. He excused himself, saying he needed to check on a friend.

He heaped a plate with fresh fruit, raw vegetables and dip, and some cheese and crackers and asked the barkeeper for a glass of chardonnay. Leaving the noisy room, he looked over his shoulder. Suzanne had her back to him talking to someone, but Travis saw Jon and winked before returning to the conversation.

When he reached Kim's door with both hands full, he tapped with the toe of his shoe. No sound came from her room. Had she fallen asleep?

But she opened the door and saw him, her expression stricken. "Is something wrong with Suzanne?" Then her eyes dropped to what he was carrying. "What's going on?"

"Special   delivery,   miss.   The   hotel management is concerned that every guest receive the best treatment possible, you know. I offered to bring this up. Slipped the assistant manager a tip so he'd let me."

Her face relaxed as she took in his obvious lie. "Want to try again?"

"Actually, yes, I do, Kim. If possible, could you and I start over? Somehow we began on the wrong foot from the first moment we met. That's made the road trip more unpleasant than it had to be for both of us, and probably for Travis and Suzanne too. So I'm bringing you a peace offering, courtesy of the fine folks who paid their conference registration fee. If it takes any of the sting out of it, I would have eaten this much again, so it's not really cheating to bring it to you."

She considered for a moment then nodded, opening the door further. He let out his breath, not realizing he had been holding it waiting for her answer. He held out the plate and wineglass, and when she took them from him, their fingers grazed. Electric shock, just like when she had taken David's car keys from him. He'd never had an electric shock from Andrea except in the depth of winter when static sparked every time they touched. He'd been amused by that, but this—this was something different.

She set the plate and wineglass on a low table, sat down, and motioned him to do the same.

"I appreciate this, Jon. I didn't eat dinner, and after making such an issue about wanting a night in, I didn't feel right going somewhere to get food."

"The hotel does have room service, you know. But I'm glad you didn't call them."

She sipped the wine, nodded. "Old habits are hard to break. I'm too frugal to call room service. Some would call it cheap. But when my stomach was starting to growl, I began to consider it."

"You need to keep up your strength, so you can sightsee all day tomorrow."

"You're right. Hence, I'm ravenous, and you've saved my life."

"Hardly that."

She took a bite, chewed, and swallowed. "For the moment anyway. What can I offer you? I have a bucket of ice and some tap water." She started to rise, but Jon held up his hand to stop her.

"I'm good, but thanks." He enjoyed watching her eat.

Her face turned pink under his gaze. "Talk about something, please. A nice ten minute lecture would work, so I'm not expected to participate in the conversation. I'd like to enjoy this lovely food without showing it to you while I talk."

He was at a loss. "What do you want me to talk about?"

She set down the strawberry she'd been about to bite into. "Preferably something without potential for conflict. Oh, I know. You could tell me how you, Travis, and David got to be friends."

He laughed. "You've opened a can of worms there. Oops—sorry, that's not dinner conversation." He settled back into the chair. "Okay, I'll give you a ten minute synopsis. Once upon a time on a college campus far, far away, there were five young men— Travis, David, Dustin, Ryan, and Jon. They came from different states and had different ideas of what life would hold for them, but the college housing department had preordained that they be on the same floor in a dorm that shall not be named..."

An hour later, Kim had finished her plate of food and wine, curled her feet under her in the chair, and still listened to Jon tell stories about his friends. The first chapters had been riddled with college mishaps and pranks. When he exhausted his repertoire of hijinks, he told her about the various states and foreign countries they had lived in or visited where jobs took them after graduation, and the annual effort to get together for a few days' reunion. He hoped she didn't notice that his voice cracked when he spoke of attending the funeral of David's father and later Dustin's mother and Ryan's sister, both from cancer.

"And Travis and Suzanne have had their trials too. Those miscarriages. So sad. Looks like little Elliott is going to be okay though. Right?" He knew she couldn't predict the future, but he'd like reassurance for his friends.

Emily smiled. "From what Suzanne has told me and what the ER doc said, she and Elliott are great so far. I'm glad she got some extra rest this afternoon, and I'm going to suggest that we both try to nap every afternoon. It won't hurt me to get some extra sleep, but it's much more important for her and the baby."

"I'm so glad you're here, Kim. For Suzanne, and Travis." He cleared his throat, decided to go for it. "I'm glad you're here so I can get a chance to know you. I feel like there's nowhere we can go but up from the way you and I started off. I guess I did something very wrong at David and Emily's wedding and offended you. I wish you would tell me what it was so I can try to make it up to you."

Her brows drew together in a frown. "You mean when you brought your fiancée and paid no attention to her? I get that you're not together anymore, but that was terrible behavior."

"Ah, now I understand. My engagement to Andrea ended a few hours *before* the wedding. It was a big, ugly blow-up to finally end an always-troubled relationship. Andrea was there because she likes a party and likes to be the center of attention. Plus, she enjoyed making me squirm. She admitted to me—actually it came out more like a gloat—that she'd been unfaithful."

No wonder Kim had treated him so badly. She'd thought he was coming on to her, when he should have been paying attention to Andrea.

He sighed. "Please, let's don't talk about her. I'm trying to block that relationship from my memory banks and replace it with positive memories. Maybe like Suzanne, this trip is a chance to make some good memories to look back on later."

"It was none of my business, but I appreciate you explaining why the two of you weren't exactly cozy that evening."

His laugh was hollow. "We got back to Nashville, and I haven't seen her since. Partly because I found another job and moved..." He straightened, tired of talking about himself when he wanted to learn more about Kim. "So I've spilled my ugly history. It's your turn to share some skeletons from your own closet."

She blinked a couple of times, as if deciding whether or not to accept his challenge. When she told of losing her mother, his heart broke for her. When she explained about her own diagnosis and tears shone in her eyes, he swallowed hard.

Eventually, her eyelids began to droop. He picked up the items he had brought. "I've overstayed my welcome. I'll clear the dishes and let myself out." Before he could get to the door, she was up and had the hall door open.

"Thanks so much for dinner and conversation, Jon. I enjoyed it. You'll think this is silly, but I'm just realizing you're nothing like a man I used to know. You look enough like him to be his twin, but in here—

" She patted her chest. "—inside where it counts, you're nothing like him."

"Well, that sounds like progress." Without thinking, he leaned down and kissed her cheek, and before he could see her reaction, he stepped into the hall. She closed the door.

He considered retreating to his room but went back to the networking event instead. He owed it to himself and the people who depended on him to do his best while he was here, but had difficulty keeping his mind on business.

He had a new appreciation of Kim and knew the sleepiness wasn't fake, something Andrea might have done to get him to leave.

Jon hoped the kiss hadn't destroyed the positive feelings he was getting from Kim tonight.

****

Kim didn't know how long she stood leaning against the door after Jon left. With an effort, she finally roused herself, turned off the light, and walking across the room, opened the drapes to look at the Minneapolis skyline. The city was beautiful—unfamiliar, surprising. She had done her research before the trip, had a list of *must-see* and would-like-to-see places.

But she'd already noticed when she and Suzanne were out exploring, instead of sticking with their intended itinerary, they'd notice something along the way and explore that. She hadn't been disappointed in any of the side trips yet.

Like the city, Kim had thought she knew what to expect of Jon. Her expectations were detailed in an invisible pamphlet about worthless men. Yet he had surprised her. Suggesting they pull off at the height of the storm and offering to drive when her nerves were on edge. Bringing dinner and wine to her, regaling her with stories when she was feeling lonely, and listening with rapt attention when she bared her soul without realizing she was about to do so.

Jon was a side trip of a sort, and she wondered if she dared explore a little further.

Chapter Nine

THEIR LAST FULL day in Minneapolis, Kim and Suzanne had their usual big breakfast in the hotel restaurant, took a taxi into the heart of the city, strolled over the St. Anthony Falls Bridge, and enjoyed the historic Riverfront District. They walked and walked before finally stopping for lunch in a German restaurant.

Suzanne finished her meal, pushed the plate away, smiling. "I already want to come back here again. Hard as we've tried, we've barely begun to explore it."

"I agree," Kim said. "I'd like to come back again, too." She held up a hand. "Oops—don't get me wrong. I'm not inviting myself for your next trip here with Travis.

Suzanne laughed. "Gotcha. Who knows when we'll get here again. The conference moves to a different city each year, and with Elliott..." She shrugged, a smile on her face saying she would be happy staying home with Elliott next year. "I hate to admit it, but I'm ready to go back and have a nap."

Kim took the linen napkin from her lap and laid it on the table, then pushed her chair back and stood. "You're wise to pay attention to what your body tells you, Suzanne. Some people never learn to do that."

"Maybe mine speaks more loudly."

When they reached the hotel lobby, Travis and Jon were sitting on one of the couches, deep in discussion. Suzanne put a hand on her husband's shoulder and he looked up. "Oh, hi, honey." He gave her a peck on the cheek when she sank down next to him. "Jon had a call from his factory and thinks he's going to have to fly home."

"What happened?" Kim asked.

Jon's brows were knit in concern. "One of the machines—it's old, keeps breaking down. Only two of us know how to fix it. The other guy is on vacation. Hiking. They're trying to get hold of him, but in the mountains, cell service isn't always dependable. I told them if they can't get him by this evening and secure a promise that he'll be there by tomorrow morning early, I'll get a flight out of Minneapolis to Nashville."

Travis continued, "Get a cab to our house, pick up his car, and drive another three and a half hours to Legend. Exhausting day—or night— depending on the flight. He's checked and can get a nonstop flight, be in Nashville in a little over two hours."

It was a lot shorter and less exhausting than the road trip they'd all expected to be on beginning early tomorrow morning.

Kim was disappointed at this insight to Jon's priorities. "It's a bit convenient to have an emergency come up at this juncture, isn't it? You jump on a plane, hop in your Corvette, and barrel down the road home, leaving the three of us to deal with the road trip." The hateful words seemed to come out of their own volition. This wasn't the way Kim treated anyone. Why was she so hard on Jon?

He glared at her. "It's not convenient at all. Without that machine running, the whole factory has to shut down. Nobody gets paid. At least a day's production is lost."

"If you say so. Suzanne? You were going up for a nap?" Suzanne looked at Kim as if she'd never seen her before, but Travis nodded and the women got into the elevator.

"Kim, you can't believe Jon created this problem in order to avoid the drive back with us. He wouldn't do that."

"Wouldn't he? Most of the time I've been around him, he's doing something on his phone, unable to let go of the reins for even a couple of days."

"He's dedicated, but he's not a liar."

"Suzanne, I'd like to believe that. I'll try, okay? Now you get some rest."

Kim saw her friend to her room then went downstairs to her own. How dare Jon bail out on Travis and Suzanne? How dare he bail out on her? Sure, the long drive was a pain, but they'd both known it would be when they agreed to come.

She pulled her hair out of its clasp, brushed it vigorously, and put it back up again. She paced the room like a caged animal, so angry with Jon she could scream. She'd been attracted to him, believed in him, allowed herself to imagine the two of them had possibilities together.

But she had been right about him in the first place. Just like Sean, he was around when the situation was convenient for him, but once you thought you could rely on him, he disappeared.

Just when she thought her day and the trip was ruined, her phone rang. As soon as she hung up, she received a second call from a different department of the Serendipity Hospital.

And the tidy little life she'd been creating since her first cancer diagnosis began to fall apart.

****

Travis went to the last session of the afternoon, but Jon knew he was too anxious about his factory to be able to concentrate on a lecture. Instead, he stalked out onto the patio and stood looking out at the city. It wasn't his fault the machine broke. Ernie knew better than to take off on a hike for a couple of days when Jon was gone. This behavior was insubordinate, but Ernie was a free spirit. There wasn't a whole lot you could do about that.

The factory could make a difference to the community of Legend, but only if it remained viable and eventually got upgraded equipment. Maybe even a decent computer system. The people were its best assets—skilled welders and machinists. Jon's focus was to ensure enough business came their way.

Kim was a good nurse, competent driver, and when she wanted to be, an enjoyable companion. Suzanne and Travis would be in good hands on the trip back to Serendipity if he had to fly out. They didn't need him. If they took an extra day or two on the way back, even the last leg back to Nashville wouldn't be so hard on Travis and Suzanne. They were both expected at work though, and that extra day might be a problem. They were saving days for the arrival of Elliott.

Best laid plans, as usual, were inclined to fail. Just like this road trip and the matchmaking his friends had done on the sly.

Jon looked at his phone. Still no news from Legend. He'd better go up and pack, just in case.

When he was walking down the hall to his room, Kim stepped out of hers, closed the door and started toward him, her face white as a ghost. He stopped as she approached, but she kept walking, not seeing anything. He put out his hands and caught her shoulders, and her eyes flew up to his face. She looked dazed. Had something happened to Suzanne?

His chest constricted. "Hey. Everything okay with Suzanne?"

One side of Kim's mouth went up in a failed attempt at a smile. "Suzanne's fine. She's resting. I—I had a couple of calls from the hospital. There's a freak summer flu going around, and a lot of the staff are sick. They were checking to see how soon I'd be back."

Jon's heartbeat began to recover. "Okay. That's a relief. About Suzanne, I mean. From the way you looked, I thought the worst. So it must really be big deal to call you twice with the same info."

Her face reddened. "It's bad to have a shortage of nurses and an overage of sick people. Not that I'm a mathematician, but the ratio is kind of important. I'm committed to stay with Suzanne though. I mean, I guess I could get a flight, but I'm needed here and on the trip back. Especially since you're not planning to go with them."

"If I leave, it's because I have to."

"So you keep saying." She shrugged his hands off her shoulders. "I'm on my way outside. I need some air." She was still pale and had grown increasingly agitated while they spoke.

He took her hand, not surprised this time by the spark of electricity at the intimate contact. But it affected him to his core, and he had to clear his throat before words would come. "What else is wrong, Kim? You're not telling me everything." He realized he wanted to help her with whatever had her so upset.

Her hand stiffened, and her eyes turned hard. She jerked her hand out of his grasp. He pulled his back, slid it into his pants pocket feeling cold and empty.

"Why would I tell you everything, Jon? If you are prepared to bail on Travis and Suzanne, why would I believe you had an interest in me, a person you barely know? Your precious factory is obviously more important to you than we are." She shook her head, muttering, "I should have expected this." Then she stared into his eyes. "I tried to give you the benefit of a doubt, in spite of—"

She didn't finish the sentence but dashed down the hall, and instead of getting into the elevator, took the stairwell. He was tempted to follow, but in her state of mind, that seemed likely to upset her further. He would pack and hope he heard from his second-in-command that they'd found Ernie, and Jon didn't need to hurry back.

He hoped very hard that happened. He wanted to fulfill his commitment to his friends and perhaps redeem himself in Kim's eyes. He just wasn't sure what he was redeeming himself from.

When the call came, Jon was even more relieved than he expected to be. He unpacked his toiletries and clothes to wear tomorrow and forced himself to go downstairs for the last night of networking. This trip had gone well for business, but he'd failed miserably with Kim, and he didn't know what had gone wrong.

Chapter Ten

THE SUN WAS rising as Travis and Jon stowed luggage and paraphernalia accumulated at the conference in the back of the Suburban, and Kim volunteered for the first driving shift. Travis and Suzanne were in the back, and Jon rode up front with her, phone in hand.

Suzanne expelled a long breath when they left the beautiful hotel grounds behind and headed out on the road home. "I've loved every minute of this trip. Except the wreck, of course. Yet right now I'd pay good money for a transporter instead of having to ride all those hours to get home." Everyone muttered agreement. "I'm sure you're eager to get back, Kim. Has the flu epidemic gotten any better, or have you heard?"

Kim wouldn't tell them about the other call, the one from the radiology department. She wouldn't share that with anyone until she had another mammogram done.

"I talked to my supervisor last night. When I get home, I'm needed at work."

Travis whistled. "That's harsh, but I get that they're short-handed. I know we've said thank you lots of times, but really, we'll owe you a debt of gratitude forever."

She shook her head, partly to dislodge thoughts of her other task when she got to Serendipity. When her shift was done, and she went to radiology.

"Please, no debt of gratitude, guys. It's been a good trip. Much-needed time away with beautiful scenery, new people." She thought of her interactions with Jon. "I'm sorry my attitude stunk part of the time. I'm thankful you invited me. I haven't taken a trip in a long time. Emily was pushing me to get some rest. So was my supervisor, who may now regret it."

They had a lot of hours ahead of them, so she relaxed her back muscles and settled in for the drive. "Last vacation I took was unique too. A bunch of ladies I'm in a book club with had a very relaxed, decadent vacation together on a tropical island. Fun in the sand and sun and all that." She pictured the beautiful Enchanted Island, hoping her mind could relax a little too.

"Oh? That sounds super!" said Suzanne. "With a book club, you say? A local group in Serendipity?"

Now she wished she hadn't brought up the topic. Jon would, no doubt, have a low opinion of the whole thing. "Actually, it's not a local group. It's an online book club, and the members are from all over."

"Really? I didn't know online book clubs were a thing," Suzanne said. "I've had my head on work for too many years, I guess. Haven't belonged to a book club in ages. I used to attend one at our library once a month, but I had to drop out. Partly because I was working so many hours—we both were—that it just felt wrong to be out that evening when we could have spent time together."

Travis interrupted. "May I interject that I didn't ask you to drop out. Don't make me sound like a brute."

Suzanne laughed. "No, it was my idea. And besides the time crunch, I was at the point of dreading the announcement of the next book we would read. Most members wanted to stick to current best sellers, and we read some gruesome, depressing stuff. I'd suggest something lighter, but my ideas were nearly always overridden. So, yes, my heart wasn't in the reading or in the meetings. What sort of stuff does your book club gravitate toward, if you don't mind my asking?"

Kim did mind, but conversation made the miles slip by more quickly. "Romance," she said softly. "We read romance novels."

Silence reigned for a long moment.

"You're kidding," Travis said. "I was sure you'd say biographies, nonfiction, something—um—"

"Respectable?" Kim hoped her voice didn't have an edge. "Whatever you think of romance novels, *guys*, if you haven't read any, you really shouldn't judge, you know."

Suzanne laughed. "Well said, Kim. My husband is like most men, and a lot of women, I'll wager. Quick to judge the contents of *kissing books*. I haven't read a nice, take-me-away romance in way too long. That's another item to add to my to-do list. So, tell me, what's your favorite? Historical? Romantic comedy? Suspense?"

The guys were silent for many blissful miles, as Kim and Suzanne discussed favorite romance titles and authors. At one point, Suzanne told the guys they would do well to read some of the books mentioned, to get ideas about romance. Travis seemed almost receptive, but Jon was a lost cause. He'd never care enough to *learn* what a woman wanted. He'd try, instead, to *tell* her.

Chapter Eleven

AT THE LAST rest area on I-65 before the off-ramp to Serendipity, Jon returned David's call that had come in while he drove.

"Hey, Jonny-boy. Do you have an estimated time of arrival in Serendipity? We're looking forward to seeing you guys."

"David, yeah, looks like around nine."

Jon dreaded the hours after that of even more time behind a wheel, although he much preferred Travis's car to this massive SUV.

Kim was still angry with him for something, and it made the miles seem to go on forever. He'd love to stop for the night, but Travis seemed like a horse returning to its stable. He wanted to drive straight through.

David broke into his thoughts. "Emily says there are two open cabins here this weekend. If you didn't know, the Standish family Christmas tree farm's B&B is well-known for its comfortable tiny cabins and the amazing breakfast served in the Christmas shop each morning. Folks come from all over, et cetera." He chuckled. "Hey, it will be a nice rest before you guys head on down the road. We hope you'll take us up on it."

Jon suspected two vacancies on a Friday evening was atypical. More likely, the cabins had been kept available just in case Travis and Suzanne needed them.

David wouldn't admit to that, but he didn't deny it either. He continued, "You're at the wheel, or is Kim? Doesn't matter. Either way, just drive out to the farm. Kim's car is here, since I've been driving it. I picked up Travis and Suzanne's too from the repair shop. It's ready for the road, but we really hope the three of you will stay tonight, rest up, and have a big breakfast with us tomorrow before you hit the road again. Emily will be giving the same information to Kim right about now. To avoid any disagreement or misunderstanding."

Good idea. Have you been watching the two of us today?

Jon knew David and Emily were just meddling in order to help Travis and Suzanne. Just like Jon had tried. And...yes, Kim too. "Will do. I'm driving the final leg, so Kim will need to give me directions." Assuming she would deign to speak to him.

David laughed. "I think you can manage, Jon. Just turn left at the sign for the tree farm and B&B. But I'm sure Kim will let you know if you don't see it. See you in a while. Safe travels."

After their respective calls, Jon shared a secret look with Kim about the arrangement. It was nice to have an enjoyable secret between them.

Her audible sigh of relief when he pulled off at Interstate 65's exit for the town of Mendacious hinted at how ready she was for an end to this journey. Serendipity lay just another twenty miles west. It was apparent that she'd be glad to see the last of him. But Jon felt the opposite. He'd misread her at first, then got to know her a little and wanted, so much, to continue that exploration. But something had gone very wrong, and he didn't know how to fix it.

Could a relationship have developed between them if they'd met in a different way? If only they could give each other a second chance.

Jon had a lot of perfect girlfriends before meeting Kim. They were perfect because he only admired them from a distance, saw their interaction with the men they loved. They were Instagram couples, attractive and air-brushed, with impossibly white teeth and problem-free lives. He had wanted that kind of relationship or none at all. The mess with Andrea aside, he had dated some nice women but never took the time to care what was beyond the idealistic facade.

Now, having spent some time behind the scenes with Suzanne and Travis, and with a few minutes of insight into Kim's painful past, he realized the perfect relationship was something else entirely. The perfect relationship was the one that was still a work in progress.

Giving up was easy. When it came to relationships, he was a pro at giving up. But staying, honoring a commitment to the other person when that was the hardest possible decision—that was what he'd never understood. His friends thought he had done them a favor by making this trip, but the fact was, he was the one who benefited by being present.

Jon had a career, people who depended on him to show up and do the work that would help the company become successful and keep the workers employed. He had a cabin up on the mountain above Legend with a view that took his breath away. And he was healthy, which meant that, barring disaster, a future existed. One in which, he determined, he would be a better human being.

He glanced at Kim's resolute profile, looking straight ahead toward home and the life she'd built in Serendipity. It was too late to make amends with her, though he ached to do just that. He ached to touch her, pull that clip out of her hair and let it fall, dark and glossy across her shoulders. To hold her, cherish her, and promise to do better.

If only they could start over with a clean slate. In such a parallel universe they'd meet at David and Emily's wedding, where he would *not* have taken Andrea, and Kim noticed, but let slide, his facial resemblance to someone from her past.

He'd have walked up to her, taken her hand gently in his, and looked into her eyes. "Hi, I'm Jon. Care to dance, and then spend the rest of your life with me?"

She would have smiled that glorious, room-lighting smile, and maybe laughed aloud before saying, "I'm Kim. You know, I think you're just the man I've been looking for."

But second chances didn't happen in real life. There was no way to roll back time, take back hurtful words, reach out in faith for what you just realized you've been starving for all along.

Chapter Twelve

SUZANNE STOOD OUTSIDE the SUV in the cool evening, her arm through Emily's on one side and Kim's on the other. "The tiny cabin is darling. I'd love to stay here tonight, if Travis doesn't mind."

Travis slid out of the vehicle, leaned on the door frame. "Sweetheart, if this is where you want to sleep tonight, I'm in. Must say though, if there's a ladder to a sleeping loft like some I've seen on TV, you and I will be camping on the floor. I'm afraid for you to climb ladders. You know what a worrier I've become."

Emily, holding her daughter, kissed his cheek. "Travis, you're sweet. We have a couple of units that are handicap accessible, and this is one of them. The couch folds out to a bed, and it's comfortable. I promise."

Jon and Travis carried the couple's luggage inside, and by the time they, David and Emily, and Kim were in there too, the place was full.

"Wow. I'm guessing you don't plan to host a big party here," Jon said.

Travis went into the miniature kitchen, smiled at the blue Mason jar containing a bouquet of daisies

"Nope. Just sleep." He wiggled his eyebrows. "As far as you know. Emily, please tell me that Jon's cabin is on the far side of the farm and that he'll have to climb a ladder."

Emily beamed, proud of the neat cabin. "Well, actually, yes. We meant to have them somewhat near each other but had to rearrange another couple at the last minute. I'll fold the bed out and get it made up after everyone else steps out." She smiled at Jon. "David can take you to yours, Jon."

That was a cue to make his exit. Jon said goodnight to Suzanne and Travis, and David walked out with him. In a few moments, when Kim had said her goodbyes, she joined them. Her eyes were suspiciously damp.

David grinned. "I am so happy to see my big SUV again. Kim, your tiny car is great on gas, but I don't know where you put anything."

Kim brushed a tear and grinned. "It's not a storage facility, David. It's transportation."

"Yeah, well, different strokes."

Jon handed him the Suburban keys. "Glad to return these, David, and happy for you to be reunited with your gas hog. We sure appreciated having it, though."

David clapped his friend on the shoulder, then looked at Kim. "Do you mind riding along to Jon's cabin? It's not far. I'll pick up Emily on the way back to our house, and you can get your car."

She looked unhappy about the arrangement but agreed. The three of them piled into the vehicle, Kim choosing the backseat. Without Travis and Suzanne, the Suburban felt empty and unfamiliar.

They went back by way of another gravel road through a forest of Christmas trees and finally stopped at a cabin that was tucked into a small clearing. Jon was thinking furiously about how to make the most of the next few minutes, after which Kim would drive off and never look back.

Kim might dislike him, but he'd learned from her. She had gone through some horrible times but, for the most part, seemed to have a positive attitude. First thing he would do when he had cleared his emails and his desk was take a weekend to see his parents. It had been too long.

He wanted a new start with Kim. But once David dropped him off and drove away, the opportunity would be lost unless he could contrive some reason to appear on her doorstep as he had that night at the hotel with the wine and nibbles.

Possibly the least romantic man on the planet, Jon had to acknowledge that for the first time in his life, he was in love. Even if Kim didn't want to hear it, he was going to tell her. The worst she could do was tell him she would never be able to love him back and he should go away.

At least, he thought that was the worst.

Before Jon was ready with an adequate speech, David stopped the SUV and switched off the engine. He opened his door and got out then glanced uncertainly at Jon. "Jonny-boy? You getting out here or what?"

Jon looked at Kim, whose face was impassive. She exited the vehicle too, probably in a hurry to get him on his way. They met David at the back of the vehicle to get his luggage. He wished David could be somewhere else for a little while so he could talk to Kim. But he'd had time to talk to her the last few days and had somehow botched everything.

Annoyed with his inadequacies, he jerked his bags out of the back. Had to jerk a couple of times because the side netting of his duffle had caught on something. Suddenly, an array of clutter spilled out of the square black organizer they hadn't bothered removing when David turned over the car because they'd been in such a hurry to set off for the conference. A couple of tennis balls, a can of flat tire repair spray, and a wine bottle popped up. The tennis balls rolled into the underbrush, David snagged the spray can, and Jon rescued the bottle just before it hit the grass.

Jon's breath caught in his throat. Not just any wine bottle—it was *the* bottle—the one he'd landed in a boot on their fishing trip.

"What? Oh man, David. You're the one who made this disappear?"

David looked at the bottle. A slow smile spread across his face. "Oh, yeah, I forgot. I thought we could have some taunting good fun with it on the next trip, so I stuck it back there and drove all the way home from Florida with it. I guess that bottle has a lot of miles on it."

Jon heard what his friend was saying as if it was coming from far away, but he was watching Kim. Her expression was a combination of wonder and regret. "Kim? You okay?"

"I—well." She licked her lips, staring at the bottle. "Where'd you get that? I know there must be thousands of wine bottles floating around in the ocean, but you know, just wondering. You haven't opened it yet?"

For whatever reason, she was talking to him now, and he would make the most of the opening.

"This was the best thing I caught when the guys and I went fishing. You can imagine how much grief they gave me when I scored it wedged inside a big rubber boot. And, yes, I did read the note." His voice softened. "It's special. But I stupidly put it back in the bottle afterward. And when I went up on deck looking for it, the bottle was gone." He scowled at David. "This weirdo had stolen it. Pretty low."

Kim looked like she might pass out, so he sat on the tailgate, and she followed suit. David's smile had slid into a confused frown. "It was just a joke."

Kim nodded. "Yes, it was. But all the others were writing notes to their potential princes, you know. So I scribbled something, stuffed it in a bottle, and tossed it into the water." She touched the bottle with a shaky finger. "This probably isn't the same one."

David looked as confused as Jon felt. "You wrote a message in a bottle?" the men asked in unison.

"Yes. Almost two years ago when I was on vacation with my book club." She kept staring at the bottle and blinking rapidly. Jon could see tears pooling in the corners of her eyes. "I never expected to see it again."

The forest around them seemed to be holding its breath. "Guess I'd better open it and end the suspense, huh?" Jon prayed the note he'd read was Kim's. It was too much to expect, enormously impossible that he, of all the people in the world, would have found the message she had written and had fallen a little bit in love with her that day on the fishing boat. He hoped very hard that something that amazing could happen to him.

Jon removed the cork. The sheet of paper, tightly bound with a red hair bungee, slid out of the bottle and into his hand.

Kim's swift intake of breath left no question.

A message in a bottle had floated hundreds miles, been found by him, and driven back to Serendipity by David, then to Minnesota and back by the four of them. That wasn't just fate, but fate with perseverance.

Jon unrolled the note and read it silently for the second time.

****

I'm writing this letter under protest, because a bunch of my friends are each writing one. And no, I don't need to hear the old question, "If your friends were jumping off a cliff, would you jump too?"

Answer: No. But I would write this silly letter.

FYI—I don't expect this bottle to be found by the man of my dreams. Though I've had some rocky times, I am not desperate for romance.

I have a great career, friends, and a life I enjoy. I'm considering adopting a pet. So, you can see, when you read this sometime in the future, I'll probably be much too busy and happy to become involved with you.

This is just fair warning, because I am an extremely honest person. If you are married, please burn or shred this note. Or you can seal it back in the bottle and chuck it into the ocean again, if you're the romantic type.

If you are not married or in a relationship and want to be my email pen pal, I might be open to that. But nothing more. I expect we have zero in common beyond a possible scientific curiosity, re:

bottle floating from where I tossed it to wherever you found it.

Makes me think, for some reason, of Star Wars. *Are you a fan of sci fi?*

Do you believe people are fated to certain experiences?

And do you believe it's important to stand by someone even when leaving is immeasurably easier? If your answer to this question is "no," please forget this bottle came into your life.

Yours truly (because how else should I close this?)

whitecapkr@...

P.S. The girls are watching to make sure I fill up the page. Otherwise I would have written less.

Like this:

Hi. I don't believe you're out there.

****

"Sounds just like you, Kim. Realistic, honest, and not expecting too much of the finder. WhitecapKR—cute email handle for a nurse."

Her eyes were enormous, riveted on his.

David clapped his hands together. "Well! I think I'll go get Emily and take her to the house. You send me a text, Kim, when you're ready for me to pick you up. Tonight, or..." He cleared his throat. "I'm out of here. Let me say first, that even growing up in Serendipity, this is one of the most unbelievable things I've ever heard." He nodded. "Okay, going."

Kim and Jon slid off the tailgate of David's vehicle. He started it and drove away.

"I have to get to the hospital, Jon. But I think we need to talk, if you have a moment."

Jon had a lifetime and he wanted to spend it with Kim, if she'd give him a chance. He opened the cabin door with the key Emily had given him, took his luggage in, and dumped it on the floor.

"Let me get us some water, okay?"

She followed him into a miniature kitchen where he found glasses and poured water from the filter pitcher just like the one in Travis and Suzanne's cabin. Kim tried to help with the water and ice, but they were both nervous and fumbled. An ice cube skittered across the floor. Kim found it and dropped it into the sink. Finally, they were on the loveseat, holding their water glasses like lifelines, and staring at the traveling wine bottle.

Jon had the note in his shirt pocket next to his heart. "I know that when you wrote this, you didn't expect anything to come of it. I know you never expected a Prince Charming or whatever kind of man you were looking for. And I don't pretend to be that. I would, however, like to have a chance for a happily-ever-after with you, Kim. We were making some headway, getting to know each other. Then suddenly you were pushing me away."

"I live in Serendipity, where unexpected things happen. Some are more unbelievable than others, but for me, this is the ultimate. If only—"

He nodded. "If only I'd kept the note when I first found it. I should have. I was embarrassed and didn't want to give the guys too much ammunition to use on me in the future. Plus, I was engaged to Andrea at the time."

She shook her head, her hair falling more than ever out of its clasp. "I'm not sorry for the time between when you found the bottle and this moment. I guess some things just happen the way they're supposed to."

The hair must have been tickling her neck too much, because she pulled the clasp out. The silky dark tresses cascaded over her shoulders, and she started gathering them again to put it back up.

"Please don't. You don't know how much I love seeing your hair down like that. Your hair is beautiful, Kim."

Her smile was sad. "I've let it grow since taking my treatments. Now, maybe I'll lose it again."

His heart felt like it stopped in his chest. "What?"

"I shouldn't have said that. I'm feeling sorry for myself. One of the calls I got when we were at the conference was a friend letting me know my mammogram came back looking suspicious. I have to have another one. Might be nothing. I pray it's nothing."

Jon took her hand, set the clasp aside. "Whatever it is, we'll deal with it. I'll be with you, Kim, if you'll have me. The universe has been trying awfully hard to get us together, and I think we need to pay attention. Whatever happens with that test, I'm not going anywhere."

His heart was beating like mad, and he hoped the right words would somehow come out of his mouth. "Kim, I know being a nurse you have a much better concept of the frailness of life than I do. This last few days I've felt more alive than ever, and more afraid than ever, too. Afraid of losing any chance I might have with you. But right now my biggest fear is that you're going to tell me to leave."

A single tear ran down her cheek, and she brushed it away. "Jon, I don't know what I have to offer."

"Kim, none of us knows from one minute to the next. I want to discover the future, as it unfolds, holding you next to me. Please give me that chance." His throat constricted. He swallowed hard. "Please do me the honor of accepting my reply to your message in a bottle."

He pulled out the note and read:

Do you believe people are fated to certain experiences?

"Yes, I do, as of the past week, and especially the past few minutes, since the bottle fell out of David's SUV."

And do you believe it's important to stand by someone even when leaving is immeasurably easier?

"Absolutely. There's no other way to live."

Epilogue

Kim unlocked the cabin door, and dropped her big handbag on a chair. Her phone started to buzz and she stopped, digging for it. When she saw Emily's name on the Caller ID, she felt a smile light her face. "Hello, friend. How's my favorite resident of Serendipity?"

Emily laughed. "Doing great, honey. Better than great, in fact. David just told me the guys are planning to make this year's get-together a whole family thing. Has Jon said anything?"

Kim remembered how Jon's face had lit up when he talked about it. "Yes, he told me at breakfast this morning. I guess they've been scheming about it for a while but didn't want to mention it until they had a large enough condo rented and everything settled. It sounds great to me, and I put in today for the time off. I was sworn to secrecy, or I'd have texted or called immediately."

"It's sweet they want us to come along. I haven't been to the Rocky Mountains before. Do you think I need to brush up on my fly fishing skills?"

Kim opened the sliding door, stepped onto the deck to drink in the view down the mountain to the little town of Legend, Tennessee. "I imagine we need to make sure the guys still get some alone time. That works for me, because I haven't seen Suzanne in a while, or you. I think she's already making memories with Elliott, but she'll need to take good video footage for his benefit later on, so he can remember his first trip to the Rockies. Isabel will come with you, I hope?"

"Absolutely. I'm so looking forward to it. Everything else good with you, Kim?"

Kim's heart warmed. "Couldn't be better. In fact, sometimes I worry that everything is too perfect. Like something bad will happen because I'm so happy."

"I think it's your turn for a taste of the ideal life, Kim. You've spent so much time taking care of everybody, making sure we all got the attention and love we needed, and now, finally, you get some happiness too. I'm so glad Jon found you. David keeps saying he's never seen a happier groom. Your wedding was awesome. I love that you went back to Florida where he found the bottle to do the wedding on the beach."

Kim flopped onto the chaise, remembering the wedding, the happiness that bubbled up in her then and hadn't abated. "There was nowhere in the world more perfect to have our wedding than close to the spot where Jon found my note."

Emily giggled. "And where David stole it."

"Yeah, well, what are friends for? It's a good thing David kept the bottle safe in that pile of junk in his Suburban. Considering Jon's decision to give up on romance after breaking up with Andrea, we might not be together now."

Emily's voice softened. "I'll always remember what you told me a while ago, right before your big road trip. Nobody's a lost cause. I'm so glad you can claim that for yourself now, honey."

After the call ended, Kim went back into the cabin to fix dinner for her Prince Charming. She would put candles on the table, open a bottle of wine. Because every single day was worth celebrating.

The End...

or is it The Beginning?

Author Bio

USA Today bestselling author Magdalena Scott writes two series of sweet romance and women's fiction. If you enjoyed Kim's story, you'll want to read the Serendipity, Indiana series, where coincidences may be something else entirely. To learn more about Jon's adopted hometown, check out The McClains of Legend, Tennessee series for small town romance in the Great Smoky Mountains. Magdalena Scott invites readers to *Try a romance novel on...for sighs!*

Connect with Magdalena by visiting her website: http://www.magdalenascott.com/

BEACH BRIDES THANK YOU

Thanks for reading Kim's story!

Rose's book is next.

You'll find a Sneak Peek in the Excerpt.

Meet the Beach Brides:

MEG (Julie Jarnagin)

TARA (Ginny Baird)

NINA (Stacey Joy Netzel)

CLAIR (Grace Greene)

JENNY (Melissa McClone)

LISA (Denise Devine)

HOPE (Aileen Fish)

KIM (Magdalena Scott)

ROSE (Shanna Hatfield)

LILY (Ciara Knight)

FAITH (Helen Scott Taylor)

AMY (Raine English)

Excerpt Copyright Information

Prologue and Chapter One from

Rose (Beach Brides Series) by Shanna Hatfield

Copyright © 2017 Shanna Hatfield

Will a silly dare lead
twelve friends to love?

Rose

Beach Brides Series

USA Today Bestselling Author

SHANNA HATFIELD

Rose

Beach Brides Series
by
Shanna Hatfield

Prologue

ROSE'S MESSAGE IN a bottle...

To the Man of My Dreams,

A crazy dare from my even crazier friends is the reason you hold this note in your hands. Under normal circumstances, I would not engage in something as undeniably foolish and utterly ridiculous as writing a letter to a man I will likely never meet. In truth, I am not convinced the man of my dreams exists.

You see, I once gave away my heart — my whole heart. The boy I gave it to (for one such as he most surely cannot be referred to as a man) tossed it aside one stormy winter day much as one might discard an empty latte cup from Starbucks. After thoughtful speculation, I concluded he was incapable of offering or accepting real love. He owns no respect for love or what it encompasses, what it means.

Love is one of the deepest, most essential human needs — like crisp, clean air to breathe, or cool, refreshing water to drink, or even a piece of rich, decadent chocolate. (Chocolate is a need and if you do not recognize it as such, you may as well tuck this letter back inside the bottle and forget you ever found it.)

In all seriousness, though, every human heart longs to love and be loved.

However, I am far past the desire for a run-of-the-mill sort of love. No, not just any old romance will do. What I seek, what I will wait a lifetime for, is the kind of love that will forever alter my life in a most miraculous, wondrous way. I want the love of a good man to add vibrancy to the colors in my world. His love should be a song my heart eagerly sings. Being with him should be the greatest and best adventure I ever experience. I want a man who perceives the depths of my soul, cherishes my heart, and takes delight in my smile.

I have no use for a man (or boy, because some men remain boys no matter what age they are) who lacks the key traits of loyalty, honesty, and kindness. For that matter, I also have no use for one who possesses a deep-seated fear of the very notion of love.

Therefore, Mister Dream Man, I care not a whit about how much money is in your bank account, what you look like, or the type of vehicle you drive. Your favorite sports teams (go Seahawks), your fashion sense (or lack thereof), and the ability to do such heinous things as burp the letters of the alphabet are of no consequence to me (although that last one is rather revolting. Please tell me you do not do that — at least not with any frequency).

My interest rests in the contents of your heart.

I want to know if you are kind to old women who hold up the line at the grocery store. Do children and dogs like you? Do you have a favorite charity?

By chance, if we do someday meet, I shall do my best never to measure you by anything except your capacity to love with abandon. And maybe your laughter. Laugh lines etched like glorious grooves of joy around your eyes would be an unmistakable sign that you are more than a mere acquaintance with happiness.

I suppose if I expect you to reach out to me upon finding this preposterous missive, you should know something about me beyond the fact I've tried falling in love and the experiment failed quite spectacularly.

The world I live in is not complex. Rather, my life is simplistic for the most part. My days are often divine, filled with sweet moments and dear friends. Assuredly, they (the days and my friends) are never, ever dull. I have never had to work at a job (at least by the definition most people attribute to that particular word) as an adult because that which I turn my hand to is something that brings me a heaping abundance of bliss.

After reading this, if you think you may hold an interest in meeting an old-fashioned girl with her share of quirks, one who enjoys sunsets, chocolate (obviously), and treasures from gentler days, please email me at OneVintageRose@...

Chapter One

"No, Mom! No way, no how!" Tanner Thomas glowered at his mother from across the dinner table. He plunked down the knife and fork in his hands and counted to ten, attempting to curtail his inclination to lose patience with his meddling parent. Over the years, she'd come up with any number of ridiculous schemes to set him up on dates, but she'd reached an all new level of absurdity if she thought he'd follow her latest suggestion. "It's never, ever, going to happen, Mom."

"But, Tanner, she sounds like a perfectly marvelous girl," Meri Thomas said. Hope glimmered in eyes the same warm shade of blue as Tanner's. She lifted a glass bottle from where she'd placed it beside his dinner plate and tipped out a piece of rolled parchment, the kind one might have used to write letters a few hundred years ago. "I have a feeling this girl is the one, honey. You have to get in touch with her."

Tanner shook his head, refusing to take the letter she held out to him. "I don't care who she is, where she's from, or anything about her. I'm not emailing a total stranger because you think she might be *the one*." He used his index and middle fingers to make air quotations. "*The one,* Mom? Come on. You said the same thing about the lunatic who worked with your friend's niece at the coffee shop. I thought I was going to have to take out a restraining order to get her to leave me alone."

Meri's smile faded. "That was unfortunate. Who knew she'd go all stalker on you?"

"You should have. Did you ever stop to consider why the girl was so eager to go out with someone? Women like that ought to come with a warning label tattooed on their forehead. Something likc 'High maintenance psycho with a serious boundary impediment. Speak to me at your own risk,' would be a good thing."

Dave Thomas chuckled and thumped his son on the shoulder before turning to his wife. "Tanner's right, love. You have set the boy up with some doozies in the past."

Meri huffed. "I'll admit there have been a few... foibles along the way, but I know this girl is different."

"How could you possibly know anything about her, Mom? She's some freak who stuffed a love letter in a bottle. I bet she is a homely, desperate, messed up chick. One who'd marry the first guy who smiled at her."

His mother's scowl made him shift uncomfortably on his chair. With a beleaguered sigh, he leaned back and scrubbed a hand over his face. "Tell me again how you found the bottle and why you think this girl is special."

Meri's giddy smile returned as she tapped the rolled parchment with her finger. "Your father and I were walking on the beach at Lover's Key State Park." She reached over to her husband of thirty-five years and squeezed his hand. "Such an appropriate name, don't you think?"

"Of course, love." Dave kissed her cheek. "But please get on with the story before Tanner implodes or combusts. The boy is barely hanging on."

Meri nodded. "Honestly, Tanner, you should come with us the next time we go to Florida. It is so peaceful and restorative at the beach house. It's been years since you've gone with us. There is plenty of room, as you well know. You could invite some of your friends and..."

"I'll give it consideration, Mom." Tanner cut her off before she launched into all the reasons he needed to take a vacation. "You know I'm busy with work."

"I am aware of that." Meri beamed at him with pride. "We're both so proud of you, son, even if you do refuse to take a penny of our money and insist on making your own way. Most young men would take full advantage of a similar situation to live a life of luxury, not work as a manual laborer as you do."

Tanner swallowed down an annoyed retort. "Mom, it's not exactly manual labor. Besides, you know working at the park is what I've always wanted to do. I get to be outside, apply my love of history, and it's awesome to see kids excited about learning."

Right out of college, Tanner landed a job working at a national park about an hour from Denver where he'd grown up and his parents still lived. In the four years he'd been at the park, he'd worked up to the position of assistant director. Every day was a new adventure and Tanner never tired of it. Although his grandfather had started a lucrative oil and mining corporation, Tanner wasn't interested in the business or lazing his life away. He wanted to make his own way and prove he could contribute something to the world without relying on the millions in his family's personal coffers.

"It's wonderful how much you love your job, honey. You are much like your father that way, determined to succeed on your own." Meri glanced to Dave again. The two of them met in college and wed a week after they graduated. Dave earned a degree in surveying and eventually opened his own business despite Meri's father trying to convince him to work for the corporation. For thirty years, Dave ran a successful enterprise. When Meri's father passed away and left her the corporation, Dave sold his business to help her with the company. Twice a year, they snuck away from the demands of Dumond Minerals for a few weeks to a vacation home in Florida.

Tanner hoped his parents would sell the business or retire. Neither of them enjoyed working at the corporation and lacked the passion his grandfather possessed in building his empire from nothing.

He certainly had no plans to join the family business or do anything beyond his current line of work. He didn't care if he made two dollars an hour or two hundred. It wasn't about the money. It was about the satisfaction he got out of his work, connecting with people, and helping them better understand history.

At twenty-six, he had his whole future ahead of him. He wasn't in a rush to settle down. Despite his mother's best efforts to marry him off, he'd drag his feet as long as possible.

"Back to the bottle, Mom. Where did you find it?" Tanner took a drink from a glass of iced tea and waited for his mother to finish the story.

"Your father and I were strolling along the beach. The sun was just starting to set and the sky burst with the brightest, most beautiful colors." Meri ran a gentle hand over the bottle. "A wave washed over our feet and I glanced down. Right there in front of us was this bottle."

"I haven't seen your mother that excited for a long while." Dave looked at Tanner and shook his head. "She acted like some long lost pirate booty had washed up at our feet."

"It was exciting," Meri said, holding the letter out to Tanner again. "When I opened the bottle and removed this letter, I just knew."

"Knew what?" Tanner asked, taking the parchment from his mother and gingerly holding the top and bottom edges to keep the letter from rolling back up.

"That this girl is the one for you." Meri clasped both hands over her heart and released a dramatic breath. "Oh, Tanner. Her letter is charming. If it didn't have the date neatly printed up in the corner, I would have thought a girl from eons ago might have written it. From what I gather, this young lady has a very old soul along with a captivating way of expressing her thoughts. I'd be willing to bet she's just absolutely lovely."

"Lovely," Tanner grumbled as he scanned the letter. He'd expected it to read like a singles ad or something along those lines. If it had said something like "hot babe searching for her soul mate," it would have been simple to ignore.

However, it was nothing like he expected. His mother was right. The girl, or woman, who wrote the letter belonged in a bygone era.

"Who talks like this? Writes like this?" he asked, reading the note again. A smile quirked the corners of his mouth as he envisioned some cavedweller crudely burping the alphabet while a woman turned up her nose in disgust.

"She made you smile," Meri said in a singsong voice, then waggled her index finger at him. "Admit it. You're intrigued."

Tanner refused to admit anything, especially not to his bossy, nosy, well-meaning mother. With an indifferent shrug, he rolled the letter and slid it back inside the bottle. "Still not interested, Mom. She could be a serial killer. A con artist. This could even be a guy, you know."

At Meri's horrified look, both he and Dave laughed.

When his mother's bottom lip jutted out in a pout, he relented. "If you'll stop all this nonsense about trying to set me up with someone, I'll take the bottle home and think about emailing her."

Meri squealed and clapped her hands together. "That's wonderful, Tanner. When you hear back from her, you have to..."

He held up a hand, cutting her off. "I said I'll think about emailing her. Don't push it, Mom. Just let it go and leave it be."

End of Excerpt
Rose: *Beach Brides Series*

by

Shanna Hatfield